A GEORGIANA GERMAINE MYSTERY

LITTLE GIRL LOST

CHERYL BRADSHAW

NEW YORK TIMES BESTSELLING AUTHOR

*"I am not concerned that you have fallen.
I am concerned that you arise."*

—Abraham Lincoln

PROLOGUE

Lark Donovan rubbed her eyes and blinked at the shadow on the wall in the hallway. Seconds before, she swore it had moved. She leaned back on the pillow, pulled the blanket over her nose, and peered into the darkness.

"Daddy?" she said. "Is it you?"

The hallway hummed along to the repetitious beat of a ceiling fan in the distance, and after staring at the same spot for a while, the wall remained stationary, and Lark grew tired. Maybe she'd been wrong. Maybe she hadn't seen anything after all. Or maybe it was William Shakespaw, the family cat.

"Willy?" she said. "Is it you? Here, kitty, kitty."

The cat didn't come.

At bedtime, after Lark's parents read her a story and tucked her beneath the covers, they always closed the door behind them, even though they knew she was afraid of the dark. Once they'd gone and she was alone, she imagined things—horrible things, like sharks springing forth from the water beneath the carpet and biting off one of her toes when she dangled her foot too far over the side of the bed.

The bogeyman was real.

Lark was sure of it.

She'd tried convincing her mother once, but her mother had just rolled her eyes and said, "You're being ridiculous, Lark. Monsters aren't real. Neither are ghosts or bogeymen or any of the silly things you conjure up with your imagination. I close your door for a reason. I don't want you growing up to be a nervous Nellie. You need to be brave."

Lark *wasn't* brave, though, and most nights when her mother thought she was sleeping, she was awake, waiting for her parents to retire to the den to watch television so she could tiptoe through the darkness and crack her bedroom door open again. She was careful never to open it too much, just enough to let in a hint of a glow from the nightlight her mother kept plugged in down the hall. When daybreak came, Lark was careful to remember to get out of bed and close the door again before her mother came in to wake her. So far, her plan had been a success. In the five months she'd been doing it, she'd never been caught.

Deciding the movement on the wall had been nothing more than a figment of her overactive imagination Lark snuggled back inside her blankets. She gave her stuffed unicorn a squeeze and began drifting off to sleep again when she heard her father's raised voice. She wasn't able to make out what he was saying, and she wondered whom he was talking to so late at night. Her mother was out of town. They were all alone in the house. Weren't they?

For a time, Lark remained still, listening. All was quiet at first, and then she heard another man's voice. It was breathy and deep, far different than her father's. The man's voice sounded like it had come from outside. Lark scooted halfway down her bed until she reached the window. She brushed the curtain to the side and peeked out.

Lark's father was standing by the pool in the back yard with his arms folded. His face looked the way it always did when Lark was about to be scolded. Another man stood next to him. A man Lark hadn't seen before. The man's pointer finger was stabbing at the air, and his face was all scrunched up.

Lark's father said something to the man, and then he swished a hand through the air and shook his head. The gesture seemed to irritate the man, and he reached out, shoving Lark's father in the chest. Lark's father shoved him back, and then the man dug into his coat pocket and pulled out a gun.

Lark's father stepped back and he raised his hands in front of him. Although Lark couldn't hear his words, she read his lips when he said, "Please, don't."

It was the first time Lark had ever seen a gun in real life. A couple of years earlier, she'd watched a man on television shoot at a bear—twice. Lark had gasped when she saw it, prompting her mother to enter the room, grab the remote control, and change the channel.

Curious about the interaction between the man and the bear, Lark had said, "Mommy, why did the man on TV shoot at the bear? The bear was only trying to eat the man's sandwich."

"Never you mind," her mother had said. "I'll tell you when you're older."

Staring at her father now, Lark wished she were older. She wished she could do something, even though she didn't know what could be done. She thought about hopping off her bed, running outside, and shouting, "Hey! Stop it! Stop being mean to my daddy!"

But before she could do anything, the man aimed the gun at her father and fired. Her father pressed his hands over his chest. He looked at the blood trickling down his shirt and stumbled backward, collapsing into the pool.

Lark pressed her hands to her lips and screamed.

The man jerked his head back. He saw Lark, and his eyes widened. He tucked the gun beneath his jacket and walked toward her. Lark knew she should back away from the window, but her body wouldn't cooperate. It had gone numb. The man reached the window, pressed his face against the glass, and tapped a finger against the windowpane.

"Hello there," he said. "What's your name?"

Stricken with fear, Lark thought of her mother and what her mother would say if she were there now, watching the events unfold. She closed her eyes and pretended she was somewhere else, somewhere safe, and the sound of her mother's voice thundered through her mind like a lion's roar. "Be brave, Lark! *RUN!*"

1

I woke to find my pillow saturated with sweat. I pressed my hands against my face, exhaled a long breath of air, and sat up, staring into the darkness. It was empty and black like a bottomless wormhole, and part of me wanted nothing more than to crawl inside and stay forever.

Ever since childhood, my dreams had been a stewed blend of fact and fiction. In college, I'd been given the nickname "psychic priestess" because I had an uncanny way of knowing when something was about to happen before it did. Most nights, my dreams were random and trivial. They didn't matter. They didn't *mean* anything. Other nights, they did, and a veil lifted, allowing me to see things I didn't always understand or know how to interpret. Tonight's dream had been more vivid than any I'd had in a long time. A young girl was running barefoot down a sidewalk at night. She brushed past me like I was invisible and kept on going. Based on the girl's size, she was young, around seven years old, I guessed. Her long straight hair was so blond it was almost white, and several strands were dirty like it hadn't been washed in days. She also had a quarter-sized tear in the knee of the pajamas she was wearing.

I reached my hand out to the girl when she passed, trying to catch a glimpse of her face, but she changed course, slipping through my fingers. Still, we'd touched for a brief moment, and I absorbed her emotions like they were my own. I felt the fevered rapidness of her heart thumping inside her chest. I felt her staggered breaths. She was scared, but not just scared—terrified.

Of what?

Or whom?

And why was she running?

The girl reached the end of the street and evaporated into the night. Seconds later, another set of footsteps thundered from behind. I glanced over my shoulder and watched a man charge after the girl. I waited for him to pass, and then I followed him. Before I could catch up, my dream was cut short when a gruff male voice called out to me.

"Gigi, you in there?"

My furry protector leapt off the bed and ran to the door, raising the alarm while standing guard. For a moment, I didn't move. Something about the dream I'd just had disturbed me, and I didn't know what bothered me more—my unwelcome visitor or the fact a flashlight had switched on outside.

He was out there, checking things out.

I didn't like it.

"Come on, now," he said. "Your Jeep's parked outside. I know you can hear me. It's colder than a polar bear's toenails out here. Let me in, all right?"

"Gigi's still sleeping," I said. "Come back another time, like a respectable hour maybe."

"I apologize for disturbing you so early in the morning. You know I wouldn't be here if it wasn't important."

I did know.

I just didn't want to care.

When I remained in bed, refusing to get up, he rapped on the door a few times, muttered in frustration, and jiggled the door handle. The door creaked open, and he poked his head in.

Luka took one look at him and went from guard dog to a pile of goo in seconds, jumping up and down until he reached out to pet him.

"You don't lock your door?" he said.

"Why would I?" I replied. "I'm all alone out here. There's no one around for miles."

"Still, you should always lock it. You never know who could be lurkin' around."

"*You're* lurking around. Should I be worried?"

He arced the flashlight in my direction, and his face went red. "You wanna put a robe on or something so we can talk?"

I assessed my current attire, a short, strappy, black cotton nightie and knee-high wool socks. On the top end I was a bit bare, but I still offered more coverage than a teenage girl at the beach. I didn't see a problem. "I don't own a robe."

He pointed at the bottom of the bed. "How 'bout you cover yourself up with one of those blankets, then?"

I sighed, yanked a blanket off the pile, and draped it over me. "Why are you here, Harvey?"

He ignored the question, opting to survey my Airstream from back to front instead. "Wow. So, this is how you're livin' now. It's, ahh … well, it's …"

"Nice," I said. "Nice and quiet."

"Quiet. Yeah, I imagine it would be. Too quiet, if you ask me."

I *hadn't* asked him.

"That's the point of being out here," I said. "I want to be alone."

"You achieved it. You're alone all right, and your hair, well, it sure is colorful."

I reached above my head and pressed on the light, illuminating the room. "I drive to the nearest town every week or two to grab some groceries and do my washing. You want to know something? When I'm there, all I can think about is how fast I can get back out here again."

He frowned. "Guess I was hoping you'd make your way back to civilization at some stage. You've been out here … what, a year and a half now?"

"One year, nine months, and three days."

"Long time."

I shrugged. "I guess so."

I'd known Harvey since I was too young to remember. On Sunday nights, he'd come to the house with a couple other guys, and they'd play cards with my father. Harvey and my father were detectives in San Luis Obispo until the night my dad was blindsided by a pickup truck on his way home. The truck had crashed into my father's car with such force it had split his car in half. The impact crushed him, and he died well before the ambulance arrived. The driver of the truck fled the scene and was never captured. It was the first time my life changed forever, and back then, I thought nothing would ever exceed the pain I'd felt.

I was wrong.

So wrong.

Harvey rubbed his fingers along his chin and said, "I need you to come home. It's time."

"I'm retired now. Besides, I have no interest in coming back."

"Maybe not. I still need you to, okay?"

"You *need* me to, or you *want* me to? There's a difference. Are you talking to me as the chief of police or as my stepdad?

"Both."

He walked to the table, picked up a book set I had sitting on the bench, and sat down, folding his arms in front of him.

"Careful with that," I said. "It may not look like it, but it's rare, worth about fifteen thousand."

He eyed the title on the green cloth cover with interest. "*Sense and Sensibility*. Never heard of it. Where did you get it?"

"A friend gave it to me. Someone I knew many years ago. I'd done him a favor, and he bought it for me because he knew it was my favorite."

"Must have been some favor."

It was.

He placed the book set on the table like it was made of thin, delicate glass. "This camping life you have going … it isn't a life. It's something else. You know it's true."

"If you're about to say it's me running away instead of facing my demons, don't bother. I've heard it multiple times already."

He nodded and stared at me for a moment. "How long are you going to keep beating yourself up over what happened?"

Forever. And even then, it wouldn't be long enough.

"I lost everything, Harvey," I said. "My marriage, my job, my … my …"

I let the unfinished sentence hang in limbo without saying the one word I couldn't bring myself to deliver.

"You didn't *lose* your job," he said. "You left it. What happened was awful. We all agree. But you can't lock yourself away forever. It isn't healthy."

I tossed the damp pillow to one side and leaned against the wall. "You know why I can't come back. Cambria is a small town. Too small. Everyone talks. Half the town pities me, and the other half judges me. I don't need it. I'm better off out here, away from it all."

"Since when do you care about what everyone else thinks?"

Since everyone else was right. I deserved their judgment. It was their teary looks of anguish I couldn't stomach.

"You still haven't told me why you're here," I said.

"You're like a daughter to me. You always have been. I worry about you. Your mother does too. I love you. We both do."

I knew. I also knew the lump in my throat had tripled since he'd arrived. I missed adult conversation. Especially his. And I missed them. All of them. "You're here about a case, aren't you? There's something you want me to do, right?"

He tapped a thumb on the table. "In a manner of speaking, yes. Just hear me out. Okay? Then you can make a decision."

"Even if I wanted to help, I'm not cut out for detective work anymore."

"Aww, hell. I suppose I should just get on with it. The truth is I'm here on behalf of your sister."

I hadn't spoken with my sister Phoebe since I'd headed out of town, which I assumed had everything to do with our conversation the day I left. It hadn't gone well and ended with her offering me a steaming heap of unsolicited advice and calling me selfish over my plans to live off the grid.

"If Phoebe wants something from me, she can come out here and ask me herself," I said. "We're both adults."

"She can't. Not right now."

"Why not?"

He cracked his knuckles—a nervous behavior he demonstrated whenever he was about to deliver unpleasant news, like telling me my house had burned down last night.

"Did my house burn down last night?" I asked.

"Your … what? No. Your house is fine. Why would you say something like—"

"Never mind. What is it, then?"

"It's your niece, Lark."

I closed my eyes.

Lark was seven years old.

Lark had blond hair.

It couldn't be.

It wasn't her.

No. I wouldn't believe it.

"Georgiana, you heard what I just said, right?" he asked.

Without opening my eyes, I nodded. "I did. Go on."

"I'm sorry to be the one to tell you this," he said. "I really am. Your brother-in-law is dead. And Lark is missing."

2

I shot out of bed and riffled through my bedside drawer.

"Why didn't you tell me about Lark in the first place?" I asked.

"I thought it would be best to ease in," Harvey said. "It didn't seem appropriate to blurt it out."

"Yeah, well, you should have just said it."

"I understand. I'm sorry."

My mind was spinning, my fingers shaking. I yanked the bedside drawer all the way out and sprinkled its contents over the bed. I picked through it and tossed everything to the side. I still didn't find what I was after. "Where are my freaking keys?"

Harvey bent over the bed, scanning the items I'd dumped out. "I know you're upset, but please stop for a minute. Take a breath and calm down."

I ran a hand through my hair and exhaled a long breath. "We don't have a minute. You know we don't. Every second we sit here doing nothing is time against us, until we're out of time and we've lost her forever. You know the statistics."

"This is different. Don't think of Lark as a statistic. She's family. We'll find her. I know we will."

He placed a hand on my shoulder, and I melted into his arms. A tear rolled down my cheek. I swatted it away, shocked my emotions were spilling all over me.

I hadn't shed a tear since the day I packed up and left Cambria.

"Let it out now," he said. "It's all right. I know how you're feeling, honey. What's happened to Lark has reopened an old wound inside you. Do you understand now why I tried to ease into it?"

"I get it," I said. "Just don't tell me everything is going to work out."

"I won't."

"And don't talk about Fallon. Not today."

"Didn't plan on it."

I broke from his embrace, and he reached out, lifting a set of keys from a bowl on the counter. "These what you're after?"

I stared at the keys dangling off his finger. They had been in plain sight the entire time. I felt like an idiot. I needed to get it together. I'd be useless in my search for Lark otherwise.

"Yeah, thanks," I said. "I'm organized. It's just …"

"You don't need to explain. You're in shock. Let's sit for a few minutes, and I'll fill you in on what I know."

I popped two ibuprofen tablets into my mouth, swallowed them with some water, and sat down. Luka jumped into my lap and stared into my eyes like he sensed the recent shift in my behavior. I reminisced back to the day my ex brought him home as a surprise several years ago after he spotted him at the local pound. The dog was so skinny when Liam opened the crate and he'd ambled on out, the scrawniest Samoyed I'd ever seen. The first time we locked eyes, he cocked his head and looked up at me like he knew he was safe. He'd remained by my side ever since.

Harvey drummed his fingers on the table. "Your sister went out of town last night."

"Why?"

"I'm sure you've heard about the fire burning in Santa Barbara."

I nodded. "The paper I read last time I was in town said one hundred thirty acres have burned so far."

"It's up to one hundred seventy now and shows no signs of stopping. It's devastating, to say the least. Your sister went with the news crew to report on it. Jack stayed home to look after Lark. They had a barbecue and invited one of the families on the block to join them."

"Which family?"

"Mitch and Holly Porter. They have a kid. Ethan's his name, I think. He's Lark's age, and they're in the same class together at school."

"How long did the Porters stay?"

"About two hours. They went home at half past seven to put their son to bed and said Jack was doing the same with Lark. At around eight thirty, Hattie Shingler, Jack's next-door neighbor, said Jack was milling around the back yard. She thought he was cleaning the pool."

"Why?"

"All the outside lights were switched on, and she could see the metal pole sticking up over the fence. She got in bed, started reading, and several minutes later, she thought she heard Jack talking to someone."

"A man or a woman?"

"A man. She didn't think much of it until she heard a loud popping noise."

"What time?"

"Would have been around nine. She kept reading and then thought what she'd heard sounded like a gunshot, so she walked to the living room. She peered out the window and saw a man in the front yard."

"What was he doing?"

"Jogging past her house."

"What did he look like?"

"His head was covered with a hoodie, so she didn't see his face."

"Then how can she be sure it was a man then, and not a woman?"

"He was tall and had a large build."

"Did she notice anything else?"

"Just what he was wearing—the hoodie, jeans, and a pair of running shoes."

I flung my hands in the air. "Fantastic, so he could be any tall male in the world."

"Hattie found it odd because there'd never been many late-night joggers in the neighborhood. And because of the hoodie, her mind went into overdrive. She thought he may have robbed one of the houses on the street."

"Robbed a house and jogged away without a bag of loot?"

Harvey leaned back and shrugged. "I'm just telling you what she said."

"I know you are. Sorry, I didn't mean to be rude. What happened after she saw him?"

"At twenty past nine, she called the police dispatch and reported the suspicious man she'd seen. We sent an officer to check it out."

"Which one?"

"Higgins."

Higgins was just about one of the laziest cops I'd ever known.

"The street was quiet when Higgins arrived," Harvey said. "He saw nothing suspicious."

"Of course, he didn't. Higgins couldn't tell the difference between a thief, a killer, or a jogger if they were in a lineup with the weapons they used from the crime they'd just committed."

"I get it," he said. "Higgins and your ex are good friends. He may be on the slow side, but he's not a bad guy."

He was a bad cop, though.

"Let me guess. Higgins thought Hattie was paranoid, and he tried to assure her everything was fine."

Harvey stared out the window at nothing, which was all the answer I needed.

"Well, yeah, he thought it didn't warrant further investigation at the time, and he told Hattie he'd follow up the next day. She was infuriated. She ran to Jack's door and pounded on it. When he didn't answer, she went around back and found Jack floating in the pool."

"I assume he was already dead?"

Harvey nodded. "I'd just rolled into bed when I got the call. Couldn't believe it when Higgins gave me the address. I made him repeat it twice. I thought it had to be wrong. Your mother was asleep beside me, and I couldn't bring myself to tell her what was going on. I decided it would be best to get more information before I broke it to her."

When my father died, my mother changed, temporarily. For a time, she was open and vulnerable. She leaned on Harvey. She looked to him to heal the hole my father's passing left in her heart. She mourned my father, and Harvey was a strong, loving shoulder for her to lean on. The more she leaned, the more endearing he became. Friendship turned to love— a different kind of love than she'd shared with my father, but love all the same.

"I assume she knows now, right?" I asked.

"She does."

"How is she?"

"A wreck. She's not eating. Neither is your sister."

I didn't want to picture it, to imagine the pair of them standing together, hand in hand, disheartened and in pain. It was too much to process. For now, it would be shelved, shoved into the dark recesses of my mind where all of my unwanted feelings and emotions went when they needed to hide. It was easier, and it was how I functioned in a state of absolute dysfunction.

I could do it.

Or maybe I couldn't.

It didn't matter.

I *would* do it, for Lark.

"What happened after you found out Jack was dead?" I asked.

"I called Crowe and Hunter, and they met me there."

Lilia Hunter was a decent police officer. She was sharp and committed. Silas Crowe was the county coroner. He was also the biggest sweet-talker in town.

"What did you find when you got to the house?" I asked.

"We fished Jack out of the pool and saw he'd taken a bullet to the chest. Looks like he'd been shot at close range. I'll know more after Crowe looks him over."

"One bullet killed him?"

Harvey nodded. "Looks like it. We secured the scene and then searched the house. There was no sign of Lark anywhere."

"She ran."

"She … what?"

"Ran from the house. She must have seen him, the man who shot Jack. She ran down the street, and his killer chased after her. When Hattie looked out the window, I'd guess Lark had already sprinted past, and Hattie saw the man running after her."

He raised a brow. "How do you know?"

"Just a speculation."

He folded his arms. My nonchalant response hadn't worked.

"You've been having those dreams of yours again, haven't you?"

I'd kept my dreams, the ones that meant something more than the average dream, to myself for my own protection for the simple reason most people weren't comfortable hearing things they couldn't explain. The unfamiliar made people feel raw and exposed like unraveled yarn. It removed their safety net. Most people were content living as sheep, following the leader. To live any other way created an unwanted, uncomfortable disruption.

Six years earlier, I'd worked a homicide case where a woman named Loretta Cox had been battered and left for dead in a movie theater parking lot. When we looked into her life, we didn't find anything out of the ordinary. She had a loving husband, a great job, and a vast group of supportive friends. Her death was unwarranted. It didn't add up.

A few months into the case, I had a dream where I saw the woman in court, serving jury duty for a murder trial. When the votes were cast on whether or not to convict the man who stood accused of the crime, Loretta had been the deciding vote, and she'd voted to convict. After the trial, she was naïve enough to share what she'd done with others. Word got out, and the son of the convicted man heard she'd been boasting about being the deciding vote, and he killed her.

When I'd approached Harvey with my thoughts on why she was killed, he thought it seemed unlikely. I pursued it anyway, and it turned out my suspicions were true. He was baffled to discover I had been right, and he pressed me on how I could have known, given the lack of evidence to support it. It was then I confided in him about the odd dreams I had from time to time, and I was surprised when he said he believed me.

I pulled out of the memory and focused on Harvey. "I had a strange dream last night. I'm not sure what to make of it yet."

"What did you see?"

"Not much. Hattie's description of the man is similar to what I saw, though. The man's running shoes were dark blue with an orange stripe down the side, and I believe they had a Nike logo."

"Huh, interesting," he said. "I need you back, working with me on this. After you left, I bumped Hunter up to detective. It was a mistake."

"She's a hard worker."

"Yeah, she is. She never struggled as a cop, but she does as a detective. Not sure why. Maybe it's the pressure of standing in your shadow. I mean, she's good, but she's half the detective you are."

"I'll come back. I'll help you. I'd do anything for my family."

The moment the words left my mouth, I felt like a hypocrite. I'd turned my back on them when I left town. I'd abandoned them at a time when they were struggling. But I'd struggled too. No matter how much they didn't understand my reasons for leaving, it was something I needed—something I *still* needed. One more day spent in Cambria, and I would have suffocated.

I saw it, but they couldn't.

"I'll work the investigation until it's solved," I said, "no matter how long it takes. I'm not saying I'm back for good, but I will get to the bottom of why Jack was killed, and I will find Lark."

3

Harvey headed back to town, and I stood in front of the mirror, assessing my current look. In a few short hours, I'd be thrust back into the throes of my dysfunctional family, and my current appearance lacked in many areas. I had large bags under my eyes, and my violet, shaggy, uneven pixie cut made it obvious I'd been taking scissors to my own hair for some time now. The boxed dye I'd used to color it was about six weeks overdue for a refresher, and my dark roots were showing.

I rummaged around the bathroom cabinet for a brush and did my best to smooth out my mangy edges. They didn't cooperate, and I lacked the time or desire to fuss with my hair more than I already had.

"A hat it is, then," I said.

I pulled a bin out from beneath my bed and opened it. It contained items I hadn't dressed in since I'd started living life in a mobile home. The musty smell didn't help either. I pulled out a black cloche hat with a white ribbon around its brim and patted it down, shaking the dust free. The hat was vintage and from the '20s, the era I was sure I was meant to have been born in. It was a thrift-shop find I'd discovered in an old antique store in New York. Paired with white, wide-leg pants, a tank top, and a long wrap, I may not have smelled presentable, but I looked it.

I turned toward Luka for further approval.

"What do you think? Am I fit to return to the land of the living?"

He wagged his tail.

It was approval enough.

I hooked the Airstream to the back of the Jeep and drove out. My thoughts turned to Phoebe and the last time we'd seen each other. I'd turned to leave, and she'd picked a thick, plastic cup off the table and hurled it at me, shocked when she hit the bull's-eye on the back of my head.

"I … I never thought it would hit you," she'd said. "I was aiming for your back."

I'd shot an irritated glare at her and kept on walking.

"Fine!" she'd said. "Run away if you want. It doesn't solve anything. It won't make things better."

She was wrong.

It had forced me to be alone, to face what I needed to face.

It hadn't been easy, but it needed to be done.

4

I arrived at my mother's home and found several members of my family had circled the wagons and gathered in support of my sister. I parked curbside and scanned the vehicles I recognized to see who was there. The group included Harvey, my mother, my sister, my brothers Nathan and Paul, and my father's sister Laura.

Aunt Laura and Paul were sitting in the front yard on lawn chairs. He was smoking a joint, and she was drinking a Coke. I opened the car door, and Paul glanced in my direction. He shot out of his chair and went inside, which I found odd. Of all my siblings, we'd been the closest.

Upon seeing Luka, my aunt Laura set her glass down, spread her arms to the side, and said, "Get over here, you rascal."

Luka accommodated her request by springing off the ground and into her lap.

My aunt laughed, kissed the top of Luka's head, and said, "I've missed you so much."

They bonded for a minute, then she told Luka to get down, and she stood. She walked toward me, and we embraced.

"How are ya, kiddo?" she asked.

"I'm okay, I guess," I said. "You?"

"I was great before this whole mess happened. Your mother's an absolute wreck, which is doing your sister no favors. Phoebe will be relieved to know you're here."

"I hope so. We didn't part on good terms when I saw her last."

She patted my hand. "Trust me, I don't care what Phoebe says or how mad she pretends to be sometimes. You're her safe place, and she knows it. She does better when you're around. She's a lot more … well, like herself."

"I suppose I should go inside, then."

She nodded. "Best steer clear of Paul for now, mmm…kay?"

"Why did he take off when I got here?"

"Seems he's having relationship troubles."

"With Tasha? What happened?"

"I'm not sure. She seemed fine earlier, and then Harvey got here and told everyone you were coming. Tasha poured herself a strong drink, and the last time I checked, she'd finished the first bottle, moved on to a second, and talked your mom into joining her."

I'd never had any problems with Tasha before. I could make no sense of why the news of me coming home had been a trigger.

"Tasha's drunk? It isn't even noon," I said. "I thought Paul and Tasha had a solid relationship."

"Times change. People do too. I've learned to expect the unexpected nowadays. Way I see it, it's the only way to live. Who knows what happened? We're all going through a stressful time right now. Everyone deals with it in their own way."

A stressful time?

From what I'd learned about Tasha over the past five years, she seemed like a decent person. She came with Paul to family events and attempted to fit in. I found her difficult to hold a conversation with because her interest in life in general was limited. I thought she was rather *blah*. She had few opinions other than her lack of interest in kids, which she refused to have with Paul, even though she'd been open to it before their marriage.

"What makes you think Paul and Tasha are having marital issues?" I asked.

"Paul alluded to the possibility of a breakup right before you arrived."

"Did he give a reason?"

She shook her head. "He's a man of few words, that one. Your brother Nathan, on the other hand, doesn't ever seem to know when to keep his trap shut. It's a foot-in-mouth disease he gets from your mother, the queen of exaggeration. Not you, though. You're like your father."

It was the reason why I suspected I was my aunt's favorite.

Whenever she looked at me, she saw him, the brother she'd lost.

"Maybe we should go easy on the sarcasm today," I said.

She studied my face and said, "I'm sorry, honey. I didn't mean to upset you."

She hadn't. Paul springing from his chair like a potato launching out of a rocket and retreating to the house without uttering a word—that bothered me.

Aunt Laura finished her can of Coke and said, "Shall we?"

I nodded, and we walked inside.

The moment my mother saw me, she rushed toward me. She threw her arms around me and said, "Oh my goodness, Gigi. I'm so glad you're here. Your sister, she's a complete mess. I am too. Well, we all are. I can't believe this happened. How could it? And why is it happening to us? Why now? After all we've already been through. What have we done to deserve it? I've offered up so many prayers today, and I need to know why. I need answers. I need to know where our little girl is."

The keyword in my mother's rambling, question-packed sentences, was the word *I*. *I* this, and *I* that, and this is how *I'm* feeling, instead of considering we all felt the same way. My mother was a good person with a loving heart, but she was a worrier, a person who assumed the worst outcome in any given situation before it had a chance to play out. Somewhere, somehow, the sky was always falling. As long as she believed it, it fueled her addiction to drama. Unfortunate events were viewed as an opportunity for her to shine, to elicit compassion and pity from others. And the worst part? No matter how many times I'd talked to her about it over the years, it was a side of herself she couldn't see.

"Good to see you, Mom," I said. "Are you doing okay?"

She pressed her hands together. "You know me. I'm a basket case. All I can think about is Lark out there somewhere with a strange man. Who knows why he took her and what he plans on doing with her? It's just … I can't … I won't … it's too much."

"We're all concerned about Lark," I said. "I need you to be strong for Phoebe. We don't know what happened or why yet, so let's not speculate."

Her eyes flickered the way they always did when I offended her.

"We *do* know," she said. "We know the man who took her is a sick, twisted pervert who preys on small children. It disgusts me to know there are people in this world like him. Even if we get her back, get her home safe, she'll be traumatized. What she was put through will haunt her for the rest of her life."

Sometimes I wondered why I tried to talk my mother down and into a rational state of mind. I almost never got anywhere. It was one of the reasons I'd left town when I had. Being around her while I dealt with my own demons had been more than I could bear.

"Where is she?" I asked. "Where's Phoebe?"

"I gave her some sleeping pills, dear. She's out cold."

"How long ago?"

My mother shrugged. "I'd guess it's been about two hours now. Best not to wake her. She needs the rest."

Gee, Mom, thanks for the unsolicited advice.

I walked down the hall and cracked open the door to the guest bedroom. Phoebe was curled into a ball on top of the bed. Mom was right. Phoebe hadn't even flinched when the door creaked, and I wondered just how much medication she'd been given. I wanted to shake her awake, to let her know I was there for her.

For now, it could wait.

I pulled the door closed and turned. Tasha leaned against the wall across from me, her arms folded the way a person does when you're about to be scolded.

Through gritted teeth, she said, "Your mom said to let her sleep. Your sister's been through enough without you coming here and forcing your agenda on her. The cop stuff can wait."

Nice to see you too, Tasha.

"My agenda?" I asked, confused.

"You know what I mean."

"I don't *know* what you mean. Why don't you enlighten me?"

She slid down the wall until she reached the floor, allowing her long, auburn hair to cascade over her shoulders. Her head bobbed toward her chest, and for a moment, I thought she'd passed out until her chin shot up. She pointed at me with a soured expression on her face.

She uttered a single word, "*You*," and then she stripped off the T-shirt she was wearing, revealing a striped, bright-pink tank top underneath. "Man, is it hot in here, or what? I mean, come on. Turn on the air conditioning."

She hiccoughed and sprawled her legs out in front of her, and I remained still, waiting to see if her verbal assault would continue.

"It's always about you, you know?" she said. "And *for* you, and *because* of you."

"What's about me?"

"Look around. Look at everything you touch. I *hate* you. I've always hated you."

"I'm not sure what you're going through, but now isn't the time to have this discussion."

"Oh, we're having it."

Paul raced down the hall toward us. He looked at me and mouthed the words *I'm sorry*, and then bent down and attempted to scoop Tasha off the floor. She shoved him away.

"I saw that!" Tasha said. "I saw what you said to her, *Paul*. You can stop with all the secret society stuff. I'm right here. Right here! Do you see me? No, you don't. You don't *ever* see me."

"Come on, Tasha," Paul said. "Let's get you home."

"No!" Tasha said. "I'm not going. I'm family. I'm here to support Phoebe. I want to be here when she wakes up. I told her I'd make her something to eat. She needs to eat, Paul."

I stared down at the drunken mess before me.

Something needed to be done.

I leaned down and jerked her up to a standing position. Then I yanked on her arm, dragging her down the hall. I got her outside and tossed her onto the lawn.

"All right, Tasha," I said. "Whatever you need to say to me, say it."

5

S he's drunk," Paul said. "I'll take her home, and she can sleep it off. She doesn't know what she's saying."

"I know," Tasha said, "and you know I know."

"What's your problem?" I asked. "I get you're going through something with my brother. I do. You don't get to take it out on me."

"What's *my* problem? Funny you should ask. Everything is always someone else's problem, isn't it? It's sure as hell never yours."

"What are you talking about?" I asked.

"You want to know?" She glared at Paul. "Go ahead, tell her."

"There's nothing to tell," Paul said. "We should go."

But there was something.

Something neither of them seemed ready to say.

She'd spiraled out, and for whatever reason, Paul and I were to blame.

"Seen your ex lately?" she asked.

It was a strange question.

"No. Why?"

"Oh, I don't know. No reason."

Her attempt to bait me into whatever trap she was trying to set wouldn't work. I lacked interest.

"You have two choices, Tasha," I said. "You can leave, or I'll have you booked for public intoxication."

She rolled her eyes. "I'm not … this isn't public. You wouldn't dare."

"You know me. You *know* what I'm like. You think I won't do what needs to be done?"

"I'll take her home," Paul said.

"You won't," I said. "You're high."

"I'm fine," he said.

"This isn't a negotiation."

"Go ahead, Georgiana," Tasha said. "Protect your pathetic brother. Protect him because he's not man enough to protect himself. Protect him because he'd rather say *nothing* than communicate with actual words. Your whole family is poison. All of you."

My better judgment said to resist the urge to slap her, to take any one of multiple higher roads. I didn't. I struck her across the side of her cheek hard enough to leave an imprint of my fingers on her skin.

She pressed a hand to the bright, inflamed area and reeled back. She spewed several expletives, and then a downpour of tears came like a broken faucet.

"I don't have time for this crap right now," I said. "My brother-in-law is dead. He's *dead*, Tasha. Game over. Whatever issue you're dealing with, *you* are still alive. *You* haven't been ripped from your family by a stranger. Stop thinking of yourself, suck it up, go home, and sleep it off."

"I … I wish it hadn't happened. Poor Lark."

It was the first intelligent words she'd spoken.

"I'll take you home," I said, "and I don't want to see your face again until you've sobered up. On second thought, I don't want to see your face again until *I* decide to see you."

Paul walked back into the house, slamming the door behind him. I grabbed Tasha and escorted her to the Jeep.

"You don't get the privilege of being around *my* family right now. Sit down and shut your mouth. Or don't, and I'll drive you to the police station myself. We can give you a breathalyzer test and go from there."

She yanked the Jeep door open and plopped onto the seat, pouting like a spoiled child. I turned back, watching Luka bound in my direction like he was worried he'd be left behind. He jumped inside and slouched down in the back seat. Aunt Laura returned to the lawn chair and chomped away on potato chips, watching the display like it was the best live movie she'd ever seen.

"Call me when Phoebe wakes up," I said. "I won't be long." She grinned. "You got it. And you be careful, now. Feral cats are even more dangerous in the wild."

"I'll be fine," I said. "I'm not worried."

"I wasn't referring to Tasha, honey. I was referring to you."

I supposed there was a decent amount of feral in me, and if Tasha had any sense left, she wouldn't force my claws to come out.

6

By the time I dropped Tasha home, she'd passed out in the passenger seat next to me. I managed to get her into the house and onto the bed and slipped out before she had the chance to stir up a fuss again. On my way out, I passed by a wall adorned with wedding photos from the day she married my brother. I stopped and inspected each one. She was happy then, staring up at my brother like he was her entire world. What changed?

I hadn't heard from Aunt Laura, so I made another quick pitstop at a place I would have been fine to never step foot inside again. I parked in the driveway, opened the door, and let Luka run free. He trotted off to the front yard, stopping to take a big whiff from a rosebush along the way. I jumped out, moved a hand to my hips, and glanced in both directions. I remembered how much I'd hated living here, on a street where cookie-cutter houses and women speed-walking up and down the sidewalk in matching track suits was the norm and everything else was not.

I'd bristled the first time my ex, Liam, had driven to the end of the street, stopping in front of this very house. I'd looked over at him, hoping he'd feel the same disdain for the place that I did. He didn't. He was elated. He removed the sale flyer from the tube attached to the real estate sign, checked out the price, and looked at me with a gleam in his eye. I knew what the gleam meant without him saying a word. The house was within our price range.

Liam was well aware the boring, tan, stucco exterior—one of only three color options for stucco on the houses on the block—wasn't my style. But it was his, and at the time I'd wanted him to have what he wanted, so I relented and faked my way through blending in with bland façades and humdrum neighbors.

It hadn't worked.

The neighbors gawked at me in my old-fashioned clothes and choppy, pink hair like I'd just stepped off the alien mothership.

The truth was … I hadn't minded.

I liked it.

It was the repellent that kept them from inviting me to one of their gossipy, drunken girls' nights.

Thinking back on how my ex had talked me into buying the place, I realized he had never been able to resist forcing a tennis ball into a ping-pong sized hole and then watching the disaster play out. I supposed I didn't blame him. Not for that, anyway. I had a big mouth, but I'd never been any good at expressing my feelings in a relationship. It was my fault just as much as it was his, and we excelled when it came to games of pretend.

"Come on, Luka," I said. "Let's go inside."

Luka wagged his tail and fell in line behind me. I unlocked the door, entered the house, and tossed my keys into the bowl on the side table. I stepped into the living room and surveyed the room.

"Are you kidding me? No flipping way."

The house was no longer staged to sell, which was how I'd left it. It looked lived in, and it shouldn't have—lived in by a giant, stinky slob, which explained why the front yard had been devoid of the real estate sign the agency had placed there before I left. No wonder it hadn't sold. In the time I'd been away, the interior had gone from vintage chic to a littered man cave stocked with empty beer cans, half-eaten bags of Oreo cookies, and empty drive-through food boxes.

He'd done it this time.

And now I'd be forced to communicate.

This wasn't okay.

I wandered through the rest of the rooms in the house and found the untidy theme had been carried throughout. It wasn't like him. He hadn't been the poster boy of cleanliness when we were together, but it was a far cry from the way things looked now.

Luka followed me into the kitchen and paused at the sliding glass door. He pressed a paw against the glass and gave me the same melancholy eyes he always did when he wanted something.

"I know," I said. "You want to go out there. I understand. Not today. I'm sorry."

I turned away, and he whined in dissatisfaction.

I stood for a moment and breathed, trying to ground myself. Coming here wasn't a good idea. I wasn't ready.

Luka scratched on the door again and howled.

He wasn't giving up, and I couldn't say no to a face as sweet as his.

I moved a hand to my hip and said, "Okay, fine. You win. We'll go outside. Just for a minute, though, and then we leave."

I flipped the latch on the door, unlocked it, and slid it open.

Luka ran for the sandbox on the side of the house to do some digging, and I focused on anything other than what was right in front of me.

I told myself I wouldn't do it—I wouldn't look at the pool.

My resolve crumbled, and I found myself staring anyway,

thinking back on the conversation I'd had with Harvey earlier when he'd said what was happening with Lark had reopened an old wound. It hadn't just opened—it had cut deep, and I was bleeding out. I stared into the water, so innocent and inviting. Deception at its finest.

Enough.

I don't need to put myself through this.

Not today.

I spun around with every intention of running back to the Jeep and leaving, but I didn't. My rage was too great. I yanked a vase off of the poolside table and hurled it toward the house's exterior. My aim was about a foot off, and the vase smashed into the kitchen window, sending shattered glass in all directions.

"What are you doing?" a man said.

I whipped around, studying him. He looked different from the last time I'd seen him—rugged, with a face he hadn't shaved for a few days and shaggy, unkempt brown hair.

"I felt like breaking something," I said. "So, I did."

"What's wrong with you?" Liam said.

What *wasn't* wrong with me?

I shrugged. "Why did you take the For Sale sign down? And why are you living here in squalor?"

"I took the sign down because … What are you doing here?"

"Answer my questions."

"Fine. I took the sign down a few months ago."

"Why?" I asked. "We had a deal."

"I know. Things have changed. I've decided to stay, which you would know if you ever answered your phone."

"My *phone* doesn't get service where I've been."

"It gets service when you're in town, which you would have to visit from time to time, no matter where you've been living."

"You never left a message."

"Didn't know it was a requirement in order to get you to return my call. And I'm not living in squalor, by the way. I've been busy."

"Too busy to clean, by the looks of it."

He walked over to the table, pulled out a chair, and sat down. "You're here now. Let's talk."

I shook my head. "Oh, no. I'm not staying."

"You won't sit with me, even for a few minutes? We have things to figure out."

"No, we don't."

"What are you doing here, Georgiana?"

"I needed my gun out of the safe in the storage shed."

"Why were you inside the house, then?"

"It's *my* house too. Does the removal of the sign mean you've taken the house off the market?"

He nodded. "Yup."

"It's going back up for sale. Please clean your mess, gather your things, and honor the agreement you made with me."

He shook his head. "I told you, I'm staying, so if you could stop breaking things, I'd appreciate it."

"I own half of this house, and I want it sold. You can't squat here."

"When I asked what you were doing here, I meant here in Cambria. You back now?"

"I don't know. I … don't want to talk about it."

He gritted his teeth, flung the chair against the table so hard it chipped a bit of the paint off, and glared at me. "'Course you don't. You never want to talk about *anything!*"

He stomped inside the house, dissatisfied and grumbling to himself.

It was my cue to leave.

"Come on, Luka," I said. "Let's go."

A disgruntled Luka took his time heading in my direction.

It seemed I'd upset everyone today.

I almost made it to the front door before my arm was jerked from behind. I shrugged free of Liam's grip and grabbed the doorknob without looking back.

"I wanted to give you something, because who knows when or if you'll decide to grace me with your presence again," he said. "Here."

He shoved an envelope into my hand.

"What is it?" I asked.

"Have a look."

I peeked inside. "Why are you giving me a check?"

"It's your half. I'm buying you out. I want the house."

It was something I never thought he'd say.

"Why?" I asked.

"Why what?"

"I don't get it. How can you live here after what happened?"

He stared at me for a moment. "We made a lot of good memories here."

"Yeah, let's leave the past where it is, okay?"

"It's true. Are you telling me you never think about it? There were a lot of good times before the bad."

I didn't think about it because I couldn't. I was bitter. Maybe I had no right to be, but I hadn't let it stop me from indulging the feeling anyway.

"I didn't ask for a divorce," I said. "*You* did."

"Are you saying it's my fault we didn't work out? What was I supposed to do? You self-destructed right in front of me. I couldn't handle it anymore."

"Tell yourself whatever you want, but that's not what happened."

"It *is* what happened. And nothing I did or said made any difference. I wish things were different between us. I want what's best for you. It's all I have ever wanted."

I could feel my emotions struggling to erupt inside of me. I pushed them down.

"Don't concern yourself with me," I said. "I'm not your problem anymore."

"Is it always going to be this way?"

"What way?"

"Are you always going to be angry?"

I didn't know.

We couldn't rewind the clock, go back in time, and fix things. It was far too late now. We were smashed and broken, just like the shards of glass sprinkled around the kitchen window.

He was right to ask for a divorce. I was a mess at the end. I didn't love him anymore, and he didn't love me, not in the way either of us deserved. We were two people who had cared for one another while hanging by the tiniest thread.

"Keep the house, if it's what you want," I said. "I just have one question."

He leaned against the wall. "Shoot."

"My brother's wife asked me today if I'd seen you. Why?"

He broke eye contact and said, "I don't know."

"You're lying. Why are you lying to me?"

I waited. He said nothing.

"You asked why I'm here," I said. "It's because … Harvey, he, umm …"

My throat was dry, my voice too cracked to finish.

Liam raised a brow of concern. "What happened? Is Harvey okay? Is your mom okay?"

If I answered based on the word *okay*, none of us were. Our lives had been cursed, again.

"Jack was shot last night," I said. "He's dead."

Liam slapped a hand over his mouth. "No, no. no. I can't believe it. I just saw him at the store a few nights ago."

"That's not even the worst part. Lark is missing. I thought you would have heard already, but when you didn't bring it up, I realized you didn't know."

"I worked a double shift last night. I'm behind on the house I'm renovating. Supposed to be up for sale in a week. Anyway, guess it explains why I have three missed calls from Higgins. Are you all right? What do you need? What can I do to help?"

"Nothing. I have to go."

"Don't leave yet, all right? Stay. Let's ... I don't know. I don't like the idea of you being alone right now."

"I'm not alone. I'm working the case, and I have Luka. I'll be fine."

"You're ... back to work?"

I wasn't sure why it was a shock to him. When it came to family, I always stepped in.

"I'm on the job for now until we find Lark, and I figure out what happened and why." I opened the door. "Take care of yourself, Liam. It was good to see you today."

"Yeah, you too. I'm here ... if you need anything."

I grabbed my gun out of the safe and walked to the Jeep thinking of the look he'd just given me. I knew it well. He was lonesome. He wanted to pull me into his arms but was too nervous about what would happen if he did. He feared I'd reject him, and he was right. I was the villain in our broken love story.

7

found Phoebe under a large oak tree in my mother's back yard when I returned. Her long, blond hair had been swept into a messy bun, and she was blinking up at the sky, watching the clouds bend and shift, break apart, and then come together again. I lay beside her and watched two clouds join together to form a shape I thought resembled a wild horse running free. For a time, I remained there and said nothing. I waited and thought she would talk when she was ready. The minutes ticked by until the silence between us became too much.

"Hey," I said.

"Hey," she said.

"How are you doing?"

"Don't forget to take the trash out," she said.

"What?"

"Don't forget to take the trash out. It was the last thing I said to Jack before I left. Not 'I love you,' or 'I'll miss you,' or any other sweet sentiments a wife should say to her husband when she goes away for the night."

"You didn't know it was the last time you'd see him."

"It doesn't matter," she said. "I could have said it, and I didn't."

"He knew you loved him, Phoebe. He knew without you saying a word."

"Thing is, I thought about saying it. It crossed my mind, but we'd just argued over something stupid. I flipped out because he gave Lark a few cookies after breakfast. I shouldn't have cared, but I did. My anal-retentive need to push my opinion on him refused to be silent. It was stupid. They were *cookies* for heaven's sake."

"There isn't a single person alive who doesn't say things they regret from time to time," I said. "We all do it."

"Why do we do it? Why can't we see none of it matters in the end? We waste so much of our lives hung up on a ridiculous ideal of how things should be, because in our own mind, we tell ourselves the way we view things is right. Anyone who disagrees is wrong. It's ridiculous. We're *all* ridiculous, horrible people."

"We're all navigating through life the best way we can. Sometimes we're our best selves; other times we're not. You're dealing with a lot right now. Go easy on yourself."

"I didn't even kiss my own daughter goodbye. I grabbed my bag, walked down the hall, and poked my head into Lark's room. She was playing Connect 4 with Ethan, the neighbor boy. They were having so much fun. I didn't want to disrupt her. She looked up at me and smiled, and I blew her a kiss. Can you believe it? I didn't go to her, throw my arms around her, and kiss her sweet face. I blew her a kiss. And now they're both gone. They're gone from me forever."

I reached out and grabbed her hand. "Listen to me. None of us has a crystal ball. We don't know what's going to happen today, tomorrow, or five minutes from now. You don't know Lark is gone forever. I will find her, Phoebe. I promise."

She rolled on her side and faced me. We locked eyes, and I swallowed hard. Her face was puffy and red, soaked in an endless stream of tears. Black makeup lines streaked both sides of her cheeks. Her bottom lip trembled. She bit down on it, attempting to muffle the sounds of anguish welling inside of her.

"Let it out, Phoebe," I said. "It's just us now. It's okay."

I wrapped my arm around her, and she buried her face in my chest. I felt useless. I didn't know what to do, how to care for her, how to ease her pain, or if it was even possible to ease it. I hummed into her ear, because humming had been what I'd done when I soothed myself on the nights I felt alone in the woods.

Phoebe remained by my side for a time. Then she bent her arm, rested her head on her hand, looked at me, and said, "I'm sorry for the way I acted on the day you left."

I shook my head. "You have no reason to apologize."

"I didn't understand," she said. "I couldn't because I'd never experienced the hardship you had. I've never had the sinking feeling that comes when you've lost all you love. I was selfish for wanting to keep you here. I see it now."

"I was selfish too. I could have let you in, could have let you be there for me like I want to be here for you now. It was a life lesson for both of us."

She turned her head to the side and sighed. "Do you believe Lark is still alive?"

"I choose to believe it," I said. "We have nothing to suggest otherwise. Has anyone talked to you about it?"

"Harvey told me what happened."

"Have you been questioned by anyone?"

She shook her head. "Detective Hunter wanted to stop by today, and Harvey told her to hold off. I guess it's because he knew you were coming."

"I know it's hard to answer questions right now when everything is fresh and raw, but the sooner I'm pointed in a direction to go in, the faster I can get to work on finding Lark."

The time had come to remove my sister cap and put on my work one. I didn't want to, but I had to if I wanted to find Lark.

"I figured you'd talk to me," she said. "I just wanted to have a moment with my sister first."

"Before I ask you anything, I want you to know, none of this is your fault. Don't blame yourself for what happened. You were a great wife, you are a great mother, and—"

"You're wrong."

"About what?"

"What happened last night with Jack and Lark ... it *is* my fault."

"No. It isn't."

She waved a hand in front of her. "Stop it, okay? I need to confess something. You're not going to like it."

8

W hatever it is, you can tell me," I said.

I needed to know, but I wasn't sure I wanted to know. Phoebe's face screamed all the things she hadn't spoken. She didn't just *think* what happened to Jack and Lark was her fault, she believed it, leading me to wonder if she had done something—something damaging enough to cast a dark shadow on them all.

Phoebe pulled her knees in, wrapped her hands around them, and leaned against the tree. "They're talking about replacing me at work and hiring a new reporter to take my place."

"What? Why?"

"There's some shifting around of roles getting ready to happen at the network. My boss is retiring, and Joe Coldwell, the man slated to take his place ... we don't always get along. From what I've heard, he has someone else in mind for my job."

"Do you know who it is?"

She shook her head. "I don't, and he doesn't know I'm aware of his intentions. He was talking to one of the other guys at the network and let it slip within earshot of Pete, one of the cameramen. Pete and I are friends, and he told me."

The sliding glass door opened, and Aunt Laura stepped out. I flashed her a look to let her know now wasn't the best time for us to be disturbed. She gave me the "okay" symbol with her fingers and said, "Luka is getting restless in the house. I thought I'd let him out."

I nodded. "Yeah, sure."

Luka bounded outside, did a few laps around the yard, and settled in next to me.

"I'm sorry about what's happening at work," I said. "What does it have to do with Jack and Lark? Why do you think it's your fault?"

She averted her eyes.

"I have a … I … there's a man who is … I have a stalker."

I sat straight up. "Since when?"

"Two months ago."

"Who else knows?"

"You're the first person I've told."

"Why haven't you told anyone else?"

"I know. I know. Okay? I should have said something, or I should have done something, or both."

"So, why didn't you?"

She combed a hand through Luka's fur. "I didn't think anything of it at first."

"Start from the beginning. Tell me everything."

She took a deep breath in. "A couple of months ago, I walked into my office and found a bouquet of flowers sitting on my desk. There was no card attached to it."

"Could the flowers have been sent by Jack?"

"They were wildflowers, and Jack almost always buys me roses.

I asked around, and no one in the office seemed to know where they had come from either."

"Any chance you remember the day you received the flowers or what flower shop they came from?"

She shook her head. "I can't remember the exact day. They weren't from a flower shop, I don't think."

"How can you be sure?"

"They looked like they had been picked by hand. I mean, they were pretty, but I've been given enough flowers to know they hadn't been arranged by a professional."

"What happened after you received the flowers?" I asked.

"About a week later, I was given another anonymous gift. This time, it was a box of candy, milk chocolate with nuts."

"Do you still have the box?"

"I don't."

"*Phoebe …*"

"You have to understand. I had no reason to suspect anything at first."

It was one of the many ways we were different. I suspected everything and everyone. Question first, trust second.

"What kind of nuts?" I asked.

"What?"

"The nuts in the chocolate. Which variety were they?"

"Peanut."

Phoebe's stalker was someone she knew, or someone who knew enough about her to recognize what she liked. Jack had always given her roses because she wouldn't be honest with him and say she wasn't a fan of them. She preferred wildflowers. She was also addicted to any type of chocolate that contained peanuts.

"What happened after you were given the chocolates?" I asked.

"He started leaving me notes."

"Where?"

"On the windshield of my car. I'd leave work for the day, go into the parking garage, and find a note folded in half beneath my windshield wiper."

"What did the notes say?"

"They were all written with a black pen and in capital letters. The first one was no big deal. It said he was a fan. He watched my newscast every day, and he had a crush on me."

She assumed it was a man, but it could have been anyone. I wanted to be angry with her, but I couldn't. She'd been careless not to take it seriously.

"How did you see a note left on your vehicle as no big deal?" I asked. "First you receive your favorite flowers, then candy you can't resist, and then a note is left on your car to indicate your stalker knows where you park and what you drive."

Phoebe buried her head in her hands. "I can't talk about it anymore if you're going to sit there and judge me. Do you think I haven't tortured myself over this already? It's all I've thought about. I'm not a hotshot detective like you. I don't *think* like you. I don't have the same instincts you do. I can't take back the way I handled it. I wish I could. Believe me."

She had trusted me with her truth, and my big, opinionated mouth had shut her down. She didn't deserve the scrutiny I'd given her.

"You're right," I said. "I'm sorry. I wasn't being fair. Please, tell me the rest."

She sniffled, wiped a few tears away, and said, "After the first letter, I started to suspect the guy had access to the building I worked at. You need a swipe card to get into the parking lot."

"Is the parking lot under surveillance?"

"I don't think so. Part of me wondered if someone on staff was playing a joke on me. I wanted to say something to someone, but I worried if Joe Coldwell got wind of it, he'd see me as even more of a liability."

"Why? You're innocent in all of this."

"Yeah, well, Pete also told me that Joe thought I was crazy. Saying I had a stalker would have made me seem even crazier. It's what I told myself, anyway."

Crazy.

It was a word I despised.

In almost every relationship I'd been in from childhood to the present day, when I asked the boy, or guy, or man the reason why things ended with their ex, the answer was always the same: *she's crazy.*

Crazy was a blanket statement, a label, an easy way to distract from the truth. He may have lied, or cheated, or spent all of their money, or had a nefarious habit he couldn't quit. His sins didn't matter, though, because *she* was crazy. Men used the word *crazy* as their Get Out of Jail Free card, because whatever they'd done to contribute to the relationship's demise, hey—at least they weren't crazy, right?

"Why would Joe call you crazy?" I asked.

She scrunched up her face and said, "Well … I may have thrown a cupcake at him, which happened to land on his face."

It didn't surprise me.

She had impeccable aim and an affinity for throwing things.

At least it hadn't been a plastic cup, or worse, a glass one.

"Why did you throw a cupcake at him?"

"Because a knife would have been too mean."

And there's where we were alike.

"I imagine he did something to deserve it," I said.

She nodded. "He hit on my assistant, Holly. He said his pants were gift wrap and she should unzip the package and see what was inside."

I felt a sudden urge to empty the contents of my stomach.

"I can see why he took a cupcake to the face," I said. "Do you still have the notes that were left on your car?"

She nodded. "They're in a file folder in my cabinet at the office. I can't show my face there, though. Not right now. But I can give you the key."

"Good. Any chance Joe is your stalker?"

"I thought the same thing, but there are two more notes I haven't told you about yet. One came on the day Joe married his fourth wife. The wedding was in Switzerland. He wasn't there. So, it can't be him."

Maybe not.

Still, he hadn't earned the right to be crossed off my list just yet.

"What did the next letter say?" I asked.

"It said he had followed me in the park on my lunch break the day before. He commented on the dress I was wearing, described what it looked like, and said he imagined the two of us together. He knew I was married, but he said since my first marriage hadn't worked out, he figured my second one wouldn't either, and he was willing to wait."

And still, she'd said nothing.

"I know what you're thinking," she said. "You're wondering why I didn't tell Jack."

"Why didn't you?"

"Jack had been pushing me to quit the station and go to work for someone else. He didn't want me working with Joe. I understood how he felt. I felt the same way about the guy. I've worked there for eight years. Eight *years*, Gigi. I didn't want to give it all up because some jerk had it out for me. If I had told Jack, he wouldn't have stopped pestering me until I agreed to quit."

"You could have told Harvey. He's great at keeping secrets."

"I tell Harvey, he tells mom. He tells her everything."

"Not *everything*."

"When's the last time he kept something from her?"

Everyone in our family saw Harvey as a good man, but one who cowered to our mother. He was the only one I'd given my location to when I left town, and he had kept my secret. He wasn't just a good man, he was a great one.

"You said there were two more notes," I said. "When was the last one delivered?"

"Right before I left to cover the fires. It said he'd tried to be patient, but it was hard. He wanted us to be together. He couldn't live without me. He said he would reveal himself to me, and when he did, he knew I would agree."

She was in pain, grieving, a complete disaster, which was why I bit my lip and didn't chew her out for being so shortsighted and naïve. If her stalker knew where she worked, where her office was located, and what she drove, there was no doubt in my mind that he knew where she lived. She'd opened the door to the lion's den, and he'd strolled right in.

9

I had half a dozen places I wanted to check out before day's end, and no ability to divide and conquer. I arrived at the first place on my list, showed myself inside, kicked my feet up on the desk, and waited. A minute later, I heard someone shuffle down the hall toward me. Joe Coldwell wasn't what I expected. He had an orangey-red complexion and wore polished, brown shoes that didn't match his ill-fitted black suit. He was the runt in his family litter, and a lover of steak, which he indulged in daily, by the looks of it.

He walked to the other side of the desk, glared at my boots resting on top, pressed his hands onto the surface, and hovered over me like a vulture assessing his prey.

It was a power play.

I bet it worked on scores of women in the past.

It wouldn't work on me.

"I was told you wanted to see me, Mrs. ...?"

"Miss Germaine."

In under ten seconds, he'd already ascertained my relationship status. Round one went to him.

Time for round two.

"You should stop eating so much red meat," I said.

"I ... what?"

"Don't get me wrong," I said. "I enjoy steak now and then, but I'm not allergic to it. You are."

"What are you talking about?"

I swished a finger from side to side. "The rash on your face. How long have you had it?"

He rubbed a hand along his jawline, irritated.

"Your lips are swollen," I said. "Get an allergy test. See for yourself."

"How do you—"

"Know? I geek out on certain things. One of those things happens to be nutrition."

"How did you get into my office?"

"I walked here. I mean, hey, if you want the full story, I'll give it to you. I parked my car, walked through the front door, and told your secretary I needed to see you. She said I could wait on those uncomfortable metal chairs you have in the reception area. I said no, saw the enormous, gold-plated placard outside your office door with your name on it, and ... well, here I am."

"*Why* are you here?"

"Several reasons. Phoebe Donovan is my sister."

His eyes rolled so far back into his head I thought they were lost forever.

"I know," I said. "You're standing over there thinking it makes sense, right? I'm the sister of crazy. Go ahead. Judge me. I accept it. I'm judging you too. I'm trying to figure out how a man like you gets away with verbal harassment."

He stabbed a finger in my direction. "Out!"

"No, I think I'll stay."

He pressed a button on his phone, and I leaned down, ending whatever call he had tried to make.

I leaned in and whispered, "If you're thinking of calling the police, they're already here. I heard Detective Georgiana Germaine is in the building. And, well, that chick's crazy."

He leaned back in his chair and cocked his head to the side. "You shouldn't be doing this. I know people."

"I know people. You know people. We both know people. Can we move on? I have reason to believe you might have a stalker on staff."

He wheezed a sinister laugh. "A what? What on earth are you talking about?"

"Over the past few weeks, my sister has received anonymous gifts and notes from a man who seems to be stalking her."

I reached into my purse and held a plastic bag in front of him. "These are the notes. They were left on the windshield of her car."

He attempted to snatch it from my hand. I yanked it back.

"No touchy," I said. "I'll be taking these into evidence. What I need from you is a complete list of your staff."

"You kiddin'? Not a chance."

"You *will* get me a staff list, Mr. Coldwell, even if I have to put in a call to Judge Masterson to get it. I'll give you twenty-four hours to get it to me. I expect it in my hand by this time tomorrow."

He huffed something under his breath. "Yeah, well, we'll see."

I scooted the chair back and stood. "I have other places to be, but one last request before I go. You won't be firing my sister, and she won't be replaced."

He grinned. "It's not up to you, honey."

Honey.

I fisted my hands but kept them at my side.

"Would you like to know what I excel at?" I asked. "What sets me apart from most detectives?"

"Nope. Not interested."

"I'm going to tell you anyway. I'm good at digging up dirt on people. We all have it, those pesky secrets we bury and keep hidden from everyone else. Secrets we tell ourselves are airtight and have no chance of coming out. I have a way of finding the cracks, digging them open, and exposing what's on the inside. Trust me when I say you don't want me to look into you."

"You assume you'd find something."

"I'd find a lot. For now, I'll offer a few words of advice before I go. You will stop asking women to unzip your pants. You *will* keep my sister on in her current position, you *will* learn to get along, and you'll forget cupcakegate ever happened. Because if you don't, not only will I scour your past for dirt, I'll expose it and make sure *you're* the one who's fired."

10

Silas Crowe was bent over an examination table, bobbing his head to Metallica's "Enter Sandman" when I walked in. I grabbed the remote and turned the volume down. Without looking back, he said, "Keep your hands off my tunes if you know what's good for you."

"Hello to you too, Silas," I said.

He jerked his head back and then removed his gloves and tossed them onto the table. He tucked his long, blond bangs behind his ear, walked over to me, and threw his arms around me.

"Well, well, well," he said. "I heard a rumor you were back. I needed to see you with my own eyes to believe it."

"It's true," I said. "I am. For now. You get some sun last weekend?"

He eyed his farmer's tan and said, "Spent the weekend at Pismo Beach. The surf was great. Glassiest day we've had in ages. And, yeah, I stayed out too long. Figured I'd suffer a bit when the sunscreen wore off. Never thought I'd look like Lobsterfest, though. Anyway … how are you? How you been?"

"All right, until Harvey stopped by this morning."

"Yeah ... I was sorry to hear it."

I bent my head toward the table. "Are you working on Jack?"

He nodded.

"Anything so far?" I asked.

"Well, let's see. From what I can tell, there were no signs of a struggle. I just removed the nine-millimeter bullet from his chest. He was shot once, which I'm sure you know. Otherwise, he's clean, and when I say clean, I mean impeccable, especially his hands."

"Jack was a surgeon."

"Ahh, makes sense." He headed toward his office and waved me over. "Come with me. I have a couple things to show you."

We walked into his office. He shuffled through a series of photos on his desk, placing most into a stack on one side and reserving a few others. He handed one of them to me.

"I haven't found much in the way of evidence," he said, "but I did recover a decent shoe print from outside Lark's window. Tennis shoe, I reckon."

I stared at the shoe print. It looked average, around a size ten, I guessed. Too small to belong to Jack. "Jack invited the neighbors over for dinner last night. Any chance this print belongs to Mitch Porter?"

He shook his head. "Hunter followed up with him. He's a size eleven. Jack was a twelve. Found a couple fingerprints on the exterior of Lark's bedroom window too, but they're smudged. They won't offer anything useful."

"What else?"

"Hunter said the front door was locked when she arrived to check out the scene. So was the side door, the one leading from the laundry room to the garden. The back door was unlocked, and a window in your sister's bedroom was open."

He handed me some of the photos they'd taken at the house, and I shuffled through them. In one, a stuffed unicorn was tipped on its side. It was the unicorn I had given Lark right before I'd left town. It sickened me to see it, to think she was alone and afraid, and I had been too far away to keep her safe.

I attempted to clear the lump in my throat. "Anything … umm … anything else I need to know right now?"

"I haven't been able to do much yet. I'm staying late tonight. I'll process whatever I can. If I find anything of interest, I'll give you a call."

"I appreciate it, Silas."

"Sure thing. I'm happy to help in any way I can."

His cell phone buzzed. He peeked at it, clicked it off, and rolled his eyes. "What about the word *unavailable* is so hard for women to understand? I mean, this is the sixth text message I've received in an hour. I said I was working. I said I'd get back to her later when I'm *not* working. What more do I need to say?"

"Not *all* women find it hard to understand," I said. "Just the needy ones."

"You still assume I attract ladies with daddy issues."

I did, but he'd said it this time. Not me.

"Don't you?" I asked.

"I mean, yeah. I've been working on it."

"Working on what?"

"It's a lot harder to find a girl who has her crap together than one who doesn't. Trust me."

"None of us have our crap together. Not me. Not you. The baggage we carry around, be it great or small, is always there. You're after a woman who's perfect. That's why you're still single."

"*You're* single too." He paused. "I'm sorry, I shouldn't have said—"

"It's fine," I said. "Don't worry about it."

I reached into my handbag and withdrew the plastic bag.

He leaned in. "Whatcha got there?"

"I need you to analyze these notes," I said.

He put his gloves back on and sifted through the notes, his eyes wide as he went from page to page. "Where did you get these?"

"My sister has a stalker. And, please, keep it to yourself for now. I don't want this information to get out."

"Oh…kay. Who else knows?"

"Aside from her? Me, and now you."

"You plan to tell Harvey?"

I nodded. "When I see him."

"I'll check for latent prints."

"Won't it be hard, since it's paper?"

He shook his head. "Not at all. Paper has a porous surface, making it easy to find prints. I'll spray 'em down, steam 'em with an electric iron, and see what shakes out."

11

I t was late, but I didn't want to stop looking. I wanted to continue, to keep going, knocking on doors and talking to people until I'd exercised all of my options and run myself ragged. But I needed sleep. When I didn't get it my mind shut down, and I became useless to anyone who counted on me. I pulled into a decent RV park on the edge of town with cemented stalls and tall, mature shade trees, and kicked back in bed with Luka.

I went over the day's events in my mind, from my brother's unhealthy wife to learning my sister had a stalker she'd never told anyone about. I thought about Silas and his comment about me being single. At first, after I left, I liked being alone. The silence soothed me. And I liked being far away, hiking with Luka each morning to places where it felt like we were the only inhabitants on the earth. I meditated. I contemplated my purpose and my dreams. I focused on what I'd achieved and how hard I'd failed. And I reflected back to the past, to my college years, to a time when I was much happier than I realized.

Giovanni Luciana had been my first love, the first man I'd ever cared about, but I'd failed to realize my feelings for him until it was too late, and he became engaged to someone else. The first day I saw them together, walking hand in hand, strolling through the grass on campus, my heart felt like someone had tightened a rubber band around it, and if I breathed in, it would burst. I was gutted, but he was happy, and I couldn't bring myself to break their union by spouting verbal affirmations of feelings I myself didn't even understand.

We'd first met in a creative writing class at Columbia University in New York in 1996, when I was eighteen. He'd started college late and was several years my senior. His sister Daniela was looking for a roommate and mine had just skipped out on rent. She'd packed her things while I was at work and flown the nugget-sized condominium coop. Daniela swooped in, handed me six months' rent in advance, and Giovanni, Daniela, and I hung out so much we called ourselves the three musketeers.

Giovanni visited our place every day. He played head chef in the kitchen, cooking some of the best meals I'd ever had. His dream back then had been to own his own restaurant, something he refused to admit to his father because his father wouldn't have approved. Giovanni didn't care. He was determined to open his own restaurant in New York City one day and said he'd call it Osteria dei Mascalzoni, which meant "Tavern of the Scoundrels."

Almost a year after Daniela moved in, I entered our apartment one night to find a man had forced her onto the couch. He'd pinned her hands behind her head, yanked off her panties, and stuck his manhood in a place it shouldn't have been unless she'd agreed to it. She hadn't. Her desperate cries for help and her attempts to defend herself were all I needed to hear to know she hadn't consented to the vile act she was being put through.

Seeing her helpless and afraid, my only thought was to hurt him the way he was hurting her. I ran to the kitchen and grabbed a pan off the stove, yelling obscenities at the man as I lifted the pan in the air and cracked it over his head, splitting it open. All it took was that one well-placed attack, and he slumped over Daniela. She thrust her hands into his chest and pushed him onto the ground. She pulled her nightgown down and got up, and we both stood there, staring at the blood leaking from his wound.

I thought he was dead.

I thought I'd killed him.

I should have cared, but I didn't.

She was safe.

And he was a rapist.

I wanted him to be dead.

I'd bent down, feeling for a pulse, my fingertips perspiring too much to gauge whether he was alive or not. I saw his chest rise and fall and realized he was still alive, but with the continuation of blood pooling onto the carpet, I assumed he wouldn't live for long.

"I don't know what to do," I'd said. "Call for an ambulance?"

Unnerved, Daniela grabbed my wrist. "Do *not* call 911. Call my brother. He'll know what to do."

I did what she'd asked, and Giovanni arrived within minutes. He was accompanied by two older, bald-headed men who dressed in all black and looked like bouncers in a night club. Giovanni embraced his sister and then bent down, flipping the man around. To my surprise, the man's eyes flashed open. He grabbed Giovanni's shirt and pleaded for help. Giovanni clenched the man's chin, leaned down, and whispered something in his ear. Then he suggested Daniela take a shower and asked me to remain with her until he came in and said it was okay to come out.

Sometime later, Giovanni checked on us. He told us not to worry. He said they'd taken the man where he needed to go and assured us both that the man would never return. I remember thinking they'd probably dropped the guy at the hospital, but Giovanni had never said where the man ended up.

The next day after class, I arrived home to find the carpet had been replaced. It looked the same as the carpet we'd had before, only cleaner, and there were no more bloodstains. Daniela behaved like the horrific event had never happened. I'd assumed it was her process and didn't shake things up by mentioning it and forcing her to relive it again. Giovanni asked me to dinner a few nights later and showered me with a huge bouquet of flowers and a *Sense and Sensibility* book set to add to my collection.

Life went on as usual. And Giovanni had been right. The rapist never returned.

The incident changed my life forever. I felt a sense of purpose for the first time, a passion for something, the same passion I imagined my father had when he had served as a police officer.

I wanted to be like my father.

I wanted to go after the vile, nefarious scum and protect innocents from the cruelty in the world. I decided to become a cop, and then a detective. Thinking back now, if there was one thing the past two years had taught me, it was that life was fleeting. It was rare to have a second chance to alter a decision once it had been made, to choose the left side of the fork in the road instead of the right. I'd spent many nights in recent months thinking about what might have happened if I had veered right instead of left.

I turned to the side and stared at a framed photo of Lark I'd taken the last time I'd seen her. In the photo, Lark held a pink unicorn she'd painted, and she smiled for the camera, unaware of the dried pink and purple smudge marks on her face. She'd been so happy that day. I'd intended on telling her I was leaving town for a while, but when I stared into her big, bright eyes, I couldn't do it. It was one of the reasons Phoebe had been so angry with me when I left. I'd made it her responsibility to tell Lark. Phoebe had every right to get irritated. I should have been the one to tell Lark.

I stared at the photo, wishing I knew where she was and how to find her.

Come back to me, baby girl.

Come back to us.

Don't leave me.

Please.

I can't take it if …

My tears tried to force their way in. But I wouldn't cave. I wouldn't give in to them.

I reached for the photo frame, and, in doing so, knocked the set of *Sense and Sensibility* off the shelf. The first volume spilled out, opening to the inscription penned on the first page.

I will never forget what you've done for my family, Georgiana.

If you're ever in need of me, you can reach me at 718-238-0935.

I am in your debt forever.

Your friend, Giovanni

I hadn't realized how much I'd missed him, missed our talks, and the fact I could always tell him anything, and it never altered his opinion of me. And though we hadn't spoken in many years, I felt drawn to him now. I blinked at the phone number and assumed the landline he'd jotted down was no longer in service. But what if there was a sliver of a chance it was?

I took my phone out and dialed. It rang a few times and then was answered by a much older man.

"Hello," he said. "Who's calling?"

"Hello," I said. "I used to go to school with Giovanni, and I thought I'd reach out to see if you know him."

"Which Giovanni you after, sweetheart?" he asked.

"Luciana."

"Right. My nephew. He don't live here no more, not for a long time now. I'm his uncle. I live here with his mother."

"Can you tell me how to get in touch with him?"

He paused then said, "How do you know him again?"

"We were in college together. His sister Daniela was my roommate for a couple of years."

"I see. Tell you what—you give me your name and number, and I'll give it to him, and he can call you if he wants to, okay? Sound good to you?"

I wondered what he'd say if I said no.

After another pause, he yelled, "Hey, Joe, you got a pen and paper? I need to write something down."

"You need to what?" Another male voice asked.

"Pen and paper. You got it somewhere or what?"

I waited.

"Give me your details," he said.

He took my information down.

"All right," he said. "I got it down. I guess … ahh … well, I guess if he wants to reach out, he will."

12

Eggs. Whenever I worked a case, I made eggs. Scrambled, poached, fried, hard boiled, basted—it didn't matter. Eggs were the answer to every question that ailed me. Today I was in a hurry to get out the door, so I scrambled a few eggs and served them on top of a piece of avocado toast. I stabbed a fork into my creation, and there was a knock on my door, which sounded like less of a knock and more of a light, apprehensive tap.

Thinking it might be my sister, I sprang up and opened the door. It wasn't her. I offered a distasteful look to my unwelcome guest, closed the door, and returned to the table.

"Go away," I said. "I'm eating."

She knocked again, harder this time.

"Come on, Georgiana," Tasha said. "I just want to talk. Please."

"I told you I didn't want to see you again until I was ready to see you. It's been one day. I'm not."

"I, umm, I mean, I know what you said. I'm not trying to disrespect your boundary. If I could just explain …"

Disrespect my boundary?

Someone was in counseling.

"You were drunk," I said. "We don't need to talk about it."

There was a long silence, and I wished she'd taken her leave, even though I knew she hadn't. I could see her lanky frame through the filtered blinds of my kitchen window.

"I don't hate you," she said. "It was an awful thing to say yesterday. I didn't mean it."

"It doesn't matter to me whether you mean it or not. We don't have to do this, whatever *this* is."

She tapped on the door again. I wasn't getting rid of her. I wasn't clearing my head. Not today.

"Can I come in?" she asked.

I sighed. "It's open."

She turned the handle and pulled the door back slowly like she fretted over what awaited her on the other side.

"Come in if you're going to come in," I said. "I have a busy day today."

She ducked inside and looked around. She didn't need words to express her opinion. Her eyes said it all.

"My maid is off today," I said.

"It's cute," she said.

"And messy." I angled the fork in her direction. "Sit."

Luka blinked at Tasha and placed a paw on my leg, showing his loyalty.

"Talk," I said.

She nodded. "I did something I shouldn't have done."

Once she uttered the words she'd been dying to say, she let them hang there, like I was supposed to do the math and figure out the rest on my own. I hated math almost as much as I hated it when people didn't get to the point.

"I do things I shouldn't do every day," I said. "So, what?"

"I slept with your husband."

I stopped chewing mid-chew. At least she'd said something I

hadn't expected, something I'd never thought about before. Liam with someone else, anyone else, other than me. I considered my feelings on the matter. At the moment, I felt ambivalent, which came as a surprise.

"He's not my husband," I said. "He's my ex. We're divorced. And he's free to do whatever he likes. You, on the other hand, are married to *my* brother."

She glanced down at her trembling hands and fiddled with the sleeve on her shirt. Her fingernails were short and jagged. She'd been biting them.

"Paul's in love with someone else," she said.

It was a brazen accusation. I put the fork down. Breakfast could wait.

"You think my brother is stepping out?" I asked. "Who's the woman?"

"I'm not sure."

"Then how do you know he's cheating?"

"He sits outside the house sometimes, in his truck. I watch him out the window. He's on the phone, talking."

"And?"

"He smiles, and he laughs. It's the same smile he gave me when we dated. And last month he went to watch a Lakers game in LA. He told me he was going with his friend Toby, but I ran into Toby the same weekend, so he couldn't have been with him."

I still wasn't convinced.

"How long has this alleged affair been going on?" I asked.

"Several months, I think."

"And you haven't confronted Paul about it?"

"Not with words, no."

"Let me guess. You've been acting out with bad behavior and too much alcohol."

"I'm not proud of it," she said. "I'm in therapy twice a week."

I nodded. "I know. I can tell."

"I love your brother. I don't want to lose him."

"If he has been cheating on you for months, there's a good chance you already have. You were mad at me yesterday. Why? Because of Liam? I don't care what he does or who with, okay?"

"I went to a bar one night. Liam was there, drinking alone. We got to talking. He made me laugh, and I hadn't laughed in a long time."

Liam had a superb sense of humor. It was one of the reasons I'd been so drawn to him in the beginning. Beginnings were simple and uncomplicated. Beginnings masked the flaws. It was only when the incubation period ended that things were exposed, things I hadn't noticed before, the nits and flaws becoming nails on a chalkboard. My flaws. His flaws. The flaws we'd created by being together. And we were left to wonder how we missed them all before. They had been right in front of us the entire time. We just didn't have our eyes open enough to see it.

"I don't need to know what happened with you and Liam," I said.

"It was just the one time. He's, uhh … he still cares for you. A lot."

And I cared for him.

I always would.

But Liam needed to make his own life now.

So did I.

"What I care about is my brother," I said. "Did you tell him about Liam?"

"I didn't. One of the girls at the bar knows Liam, and she saw us leave together. She told Paul."

"Let me guess—was it Tracy Rhodes?"

She nodded.

"Tracy tattled because she's always had a crush on Liam but lacks the nerve to act on it. What did my brother say?"

"He just said he knew. That was it."

"Have you tried talking to him again?"

"I don't know what to say."

Anything. Say anything.

"You're an adult, Tasha. Start acting like one. You need to get this all out into the open. The fear you have about it won't change the outcome, so you may as well talk it out. You can't remain in limbo. It isn't fair to either one of you."

Look at me, a modern-day Dear Abby.

I was the last person who should have been giving advice.

She leaned back and crossed her arms like she wasn't going anywhere anytime soon. I was restive, and my eggs were getting cold.

"Anything else?" I asked.

"I guess not."

"All right. I'll see you later, then."

She stood, dug into her purse, and set a decent bottle of red wine on the counter.

"What's this?" I asked.

"A peace offering," she said. "If you ever want to talk to *me* about anything, I'm here for you. It might help to have a conversation about what happened before you left. Just a suggestion."

I pushed the eggs to the side, leaned over, and opened the door. "I've made peace with it. I don't need to talk to anyone."

13

Joseph Coldwell's secretary called to say she had the list of names I'd requested at the news station, and she asked for my email address. I gave it to her. She also said Joseph wanted her to pass along a message, which I could tell by the tone of her voice wasn't a message she was comfortable sharing.

The message was: This concludes our business, Detective Germaine.

Maybe it did.

Maybe it didn't.

I called Silas to check in. He had pulled several prints off the notes I'd given him. Most were partials, and more than half were smaller and belonged to my sister. But there was one thumb print he was excited about. I asked him to wait an hour and then send the results to Harvey. I needed to talk to Harvey first.

It was quiet at the police station when I arrived. I scanned the room for any signs of intelligent life. The phone rang in the office next to where I stood. I pushed the door open. The room was empty.

"They're not here," Harvey said as he swept past, "and you're late."

"Late for what?"

"The briefing."

"I wasn't aware of a briefing."

"Check your messages."

I picked my phone out of my bag and clicked on the screen. Nothing happened. I switched it off and fired it up again. Still nothing.

"You gonna fiddle with your phone all morning, or are you going to join us?" he asked.

"Sorry, something's wrong with it."

I slipped it back into my purse and followed him into a room. The moment I stepped inside, I was met with shocked stares and lingering whispers. It was what I'd left town to avoid—the stares, the whispers, the opinions. Everyone was my harshest critic.

Harvey glanced at me, and then at the curious crowd, and said, "Yesterday, I made you all aware Detective Germaine would be joining us on this case. Let's make her feel welcome. We're lucky to have her back."

His declaration drew some weak smiles from the crowd as well as some overexcited ones. My eyes fell on Lilia Hunter, who turned away the moment my focus shifted to her. I wondered how she felt about being demoted to her old job while I took back mine. If I were her, I would have contemplated revenge. Whatever she was feeling, she had every right to feel it.

I took a seat at the back of the class and waited for Harvey to begin.

"Just want to bring you all up to speed on where we're at," he said.

He attached several photos to the whiteboard and explained what they were and how they were relevant to the case. The photos were the same ones Silas had shown me the day before. Nothing new there.

Then he discussed a possible lead, a neighbor on the next street who'd said he saw a car speed down the road around the time of Jack's murder. Harvey was sending Hunter to follow up. He closed with a photo I hadn't seen before, a photo of a young girl, one of Jack's patients. Her name was Everly Navarro, and she'd been born with only one lung. Jack had performed an experimental surgery on her, a stem cell-engineered trachea transplant. He'd told her parents there was a good chance her airway would give up without the procedure, and they'd signed off on it. Weeks after the surgery, Everly died when her trachea collapsed. She suffocated and experienced fatal brain damage. Her parents were furious. They sued, but so far, no judgment had been reached.

I remembered Phoebe telling me about the case. At the time, she worried it would ruin Jack's reputation in the city. Jack was a fearless guy. A confident guy. Not only was he sure he wouldn't be found guilty, he'd planned to attempt the surgery again in the future.

Harvey announced I would follow up with Everly Navarro's parents, and the meeting was adjourned. Higgins made a beeline in my direction, but I blew him off. My attention was on Hunter, who grabbed her cell phone off the table and brushed by me without saying a word.

I caught up to her and said, "Hey, can I talk to you for a minute?"

She considered the request. "Yeah, I guess."

We walked to my office, which I wasn't sure was even still mine —until we walked in. I found it had been preserved, frozen in time from the last day I was there. Even my black, vintage, beaded clutch was still hanging from the hook on the back of the door.

"Huh," I said. "I thought he'd give my office to someone else."

"He hoped you'd come back one day," she said. "Looks like he got what he wanted."

She sat down. I remained standing.

"You're mad at me," I said. "I get it. I'd be mad too."

"I'm not mad at you. I'm mad at myself."

"Why?"

"Because I was relieved when I heard you were back."

It wasn't anger she felt. It was guilt. I was all too familiar with the feeling.

"There's nothing wrong with feeling that way."

She leaned back in the chair and shook her head. "Isn't there? I've aspired to become a detective for years. Then it was handed to me, and I hate it. I mean, hate is a stronger word than I should use, I guess. It feels like I've let everyone down, and it's embarrassing, being demoted instead of promoted. No one looks at me the same, and the thing is, they didn't look at me the same when I made detective, either. It was like they all knew it wouldn't last."

"What do you want?"

She narrowed her eyes. "I'm not sure what you mean."

"What are you passionate about? If you could do anything, be anything, what would it be? Would it still be a job on the police force? Or would it be something else?"

"I'd still be doing this." She paused. "Actually, no. It's not true. I wouldn't. I like helping people, but this case, it's too much pressure."

"Good," I said.

"Good?"

"You've taken the first step to becoming true to yourself. Now you need to figure out what you want to do. Just do me a favor and wait until after this case is solved, all right? It's selfish of me, but I need all the help I can get."

She nodded. "Sure. And, hey, thanks for the chat. I'm glad you're back."

And relieved.

I could tell.

I'd put out one fire and set off to start another. I left my office and walked to Harvey's.

"I need to tell you something about Phoebe," I said.

Harvey offered a slight nod and motioned for me to sit down. I shut his office door and took a seat.

"What I'm about to tell you can't leave this room," I said. "Mom isn't to know. I'm aware you don't like keeping things from her, but this isn't our secret to tell."

He leaned back, entwined his fingers behind his head, and squinted at me. "Mmmph. How bad of a secret are we talking here?"

"Do I have your word?"

The silence lasted so long I thought he might say no.

"Of course," he said. "You'd never put me in this position if it wasn't necessary."

I breathed a sigh of relief and filled him in on Phoebe's stalker, the notes she'd received, and my visit with Joseph Coldwell.

When I finished, he scratched his forehead and said, "I never liked him. Coldwell. Never liked the idea of her working with him, either. Thinks he's better than everyone else. He isn't. I still remember when he was a scrawny, doe-eyed kid in high school. He was a punk then, and he's a punk now."

It wasn't like Harvey to speak ill of others, and I assumed there must have been something more between the two of them, something he didn't want to share.

I handed Harvey what Coldwell's secretary had sent over. "Here's a list of all the employees working at the news station. When Silas sends you the thumb print, I need to have it run through AFIS to see if any of these guys are a match. Until then, I'm off to see what else I can dig up."

14

I dropped my impaired cell phone off for emergency surgery and stopped at Jack's office in San Luis Obispo to do a bit of reconnaissance. Terry Pearson was a fellow surgeon who shared an office building with Jack. If anyone knew about the Navarro case, he did, or Shane Curtis did, the assistant they had both shared.

Shane's face was glued to his cell phone when I walked in, and he didn't notice me, even though I was right in front of his desk.

"Hello," I said. "Whatcha doing?"

Shane glanced up and stared at me through thick, black-rimmed glasses. He flipped the phone around and showed me the distraction.

"You're playing video games?" I said. "Shouldn't you be working?"

He gestured toward the waiting room as if to prove a point.

It was empty.

"Have you ever played Fortnite?" he asked.

I shook my head and took a seat.

"You should check it out," he said. "It's addicting."

"I don't have time for games."

I also found them to be a colossal waste of time.

But what did I know?

The confused expression on Shane's face made me feel like my anti-gaming proclamation had been spoken in a foreign language, one he didn't understand.

"You serious?" he asked. "You *never* play games on your phone? Not one?"

"Does the *New York Times* Crossword count?"

He squinted. "The ... what?"

"You know what a crossword puzzle is, right?"

"I mean, yeah. It just sounds ... umm ... like something an old—"

I flattened my hands on top of the desk and leaned in. "Watch yourself."

He sunk into his chair and frowned. Then he clicked his phone off and set it on the desk.

"You look familiar," he said. "Have you been here before?"

"I'm Phoebe Donovan's sister."

The fact we were sisters wasn't the reason he recognized me.

He just hadn't connected the dots yet.

"How is Phoebe?" he asked. "I tried to call her this morning, but she didn't answer. I've been meaning to get her some flowers, but I'm no good at picking out that stuff."

It was possible Shane had never been in a serious relationship before. He was in his early thirties, donned a mouthful of braces, and sported a conservative look that said he'd aspired to his position of Grand Office Pencil Pusher and would be satisfied to remain in the role for the remainder of his life.

"Flowers would be nice," I said. "Phoebe needs all the support she can get right now."

"I'm sorry about what happened. Doctor Donovan was a great guy to work for, and Lark's a great kid. Wherever she is, I hope she's okay."

"I stopped by to talk to you about Everly Navarro."

He nodded. "Oh. Okay."

"What kind of people are Everly's parents?"

"What do you mean?"

"Do you think Everly Navarro's father is the type of guy who would seek revenge for his daughter's death?"

Shane tapped his finger on the desk and gave the question some thought. "I mean, maybe. Why? What makes you—"

"I'm not just Phoebe's sister. I'm a detective. I'm working the case."

He blinked at me and there it was—recognition. He realized where he'd seen me before. He slumped in his chair and tried to act nonchalant, like the light-bulb moment had changed nothing, but his face said it all.

He cleared his throat, not once, but twice, and said, "From what Jack told me, Everly Navarro's father never talked much when they met, before or after the surgery. Everly's mother did most of the talking. Hard to know what's going through her father's mind. They say people like him, the quiet, calculating ones, are capable of anything."

"*Who* says?" I asked.

"Profilers. You know, guys like The Rostov Ripper."

"Andrei Chikatilo?"

He nodded. "The guy was awkward and shy, and he murdered over fifty people. He killed women and kids, and get this, he had a wife and kids of his own. It didn't stop him. His family had no idea. No one did. Not for a long time."

"Seems you have an interest in serial killers," I said.

"I mean, I binge watch *Murderous Minds* sometimes. You ever seen it?"

I had.

Every episode.

It was to me what gaming was to him.

"Tell me more about Everly's mother," I said.

"I liked her at first. She was nice. A week before the surgery, she brought in a bunch of frosted, heart-shaped sugar cookies she'd baked to thank Jack for everything he'd done for Everly. After Everly died though, she changed."

"Makes sense. The woman lost her daughter."

"She was angry. She egged our office building one night and then left a message and admitted she'd done it."

"Did Jack do anything about it?"

Shane shook his head. "Nope. He hired cleaners to clean it up. He felt bad about Everly's death and said he'd let them all down. He thought her mother had lashed out because she was suffering. He figured she'd get her anger out and then she'd move on."

"She didn't move on, though," I said. "She sued him."

"Yeah, *after* she slashed his tires and poured honey all over his new Mercedes. I get how mad she was at him, but who does that?"

Someone who was suffering.

"Did Phoebe know about any of this?" I asked.

He shook his head. "She knew he'd been sued, but he didn't want to worry her, so he didn't mention the other stuff."

The more I delved into Jack and Phoebe's relationship, the more I realized they'd both kept secrets from each other.

"What was Jack's reaction when he found out he'd been sued?" I asked.

"Part of him wanted to pay them off, not in the amount they wanted, but an offer substantial enough to appease them. The other part of him felt he'd been clear when he explained the risks of the surgery. They knew it might not be a success. They just wouldn't allow themselves to believe anything other than the outcome they wanted."

I nodded. "Thanks for the information, Shane. Anything else I should know?"

"I didn't believe Everly's mother would have let Jack off the hook whether she received a settlement or not."

"Why not?"

Shane opened his laptop, typed in a few things, and then said, "Come look at this."

I walked around to his side of the desk and leaned in, surprised to see Jack had received emails from Everly's mother every day beginning a week after Everly's death. There was never a message, just an attached photo of Everly. A different one had been sent each day, starting with Everly's baby pictures and going all the way up to Everly in the casket on the day of her funeral. The email address was a Gmail account in the name of Lenore Navarro, but it didn't mean Lenore had been the one sending the emails. The emails could have been Everly's father's way of dealing with his daughter's death.

"What did Jack say about the emails?" I asked.

"Nothing for the first few weeks, and then he asked me to mark them as spam. Even after I did, I noticed they were opened. Jack looked at them."

"Where is Doctor Pearson today?"

"It's his day off. I can give you his number, though."

I nodded, and Shane scribbled it down on a piece of paper and handed it to me. I reached for it, and he didn't let go.

"Is there something else?" I asked.

"One thing. Jack hired a private investigator."

"When?"

"About a month ago. I only know because the PI came in, and they talked in Jack's office. After the guy left, I went into Jack's office to give him his phone messages, and the guy's card was on his desk."

"You have a name?"

"Andy Sanders."

"Any idea why Jack hired him?"

"I'm not sure, but after their meeting, when Jack opened the door, I heard him say he didn't know what he'd do if it turned out to be true."

If *what* turned out to be true?

15

I returned to the repair shop to discover my phone had died. I bought a new one, which ate up precious time in my day, and I gave Terry Pearson a call. I explained who I was and questioned him about Everly Navarro. He told me he was heading to the office to pick up a file he needed and suggested we meet there in thirty minutes. I did a U-turn and headed over.

Several minutes later, I followed a restored, mint-green pickup truck into the office parking lot. I pulled my car alongside and got out, eyeing the man who'd just exited the truck. He had short, auburn hair and was dressed in a blue-and-white striped polo shirt and dark slacks. With the exception of a thin, silver hoop earring dangling from his ear, his appearance was polished.

"Terry Pearson?" I asked.

He nodded.

"Nice truck," I said. "Ford F100, right?"

"Yeah, good call."

"I'm guessing it's a '58 model?"

"It's a '56." He smiled. "You know your classics."

I tried to refrain from running my hand along the truck's sheen metal exterior and failed. It was like a magnificent, shiny piece of kryptonite, and I couldn't resist.

"I own an older model vehicle myself," I said.

Terry raised a brow and inspected my Jeep as if to suggest I considered it to be a model worth talking about.

"The Jeep's, uh ... I just use it to pull my Airstream," I said.

"Ahh, what else do you drive?"

"I own a 1937 Jaguar SS 100. It's white with a blood-red interior."

I could have gone a lot more basic and said the interior was dark red, or crimson even, but something about the words "blood red" delivered the perfect visual imagery—in my mind, at least.

He blew a long whistle and said, "If it's the car I'm thinking it is, I can't believe you're not driving it around, showing it off."

"I didn't buy it to show off. It belonged to my grandfather."

"Still, you shouldn't keep a beauty like that locked up when it could be on the road."

He was right.

Before I'd left town, it had been my daily driver.

Cambria was small, home to a mere six thousand residents, and everyone knew I owned it. It was the kind of attention I'd never cared about in the past but shied away from now.

His expression soured. "I just stopped at your mother's place and visited with Phoebe. I'd like to offer my help in any way I can. I offered to take care of Jack's funeral arrangements or to help with them, at least, but your mother interjected and assured me it had already been handled."

I had the feeling it *hadn't* been handled yet. Mom just wasn't about to allow Terry's lightning to steal her thunder.

"My mother tends to take over in these kinds of situations," I said. "Thanks for the offer to help. I appreciate it, and I'm sure Phoebe does too."

"You have any leads on the investigation yet?"

"A few," I said.

"How can I help?"

I appreciated his candor and eagerness to get straight to the point.

"What can you tell me about Everly Navarro and her parents?" I asked.

He tucked his hands inside his pockets, leaned against the truck, and pondered the question. "I didn't have much interaction with them. I saw them a couple of times before Jack performed Everly's surgery, and that was about it. Shame about what happened. There were risks associated with the surgery Jack performed on their daughter. The Navarros were well aware of those when they elected to go through with it."

"What do you know about the emails Jack received?" I asked.

He raised a brow. "I'm not sure what you're asking."

His innocent expression seemed genuine.

Maybe he didn't know about the emails.

"After Everly died, daily emails were sent to Jack from an account in the name of Lenore Navarro," I said.

"I didn't know they'd been in touch with him. The only correspondence I was aware of was some of the back-and-forth messages between Jack and his lawyer regarding the lawsuit."

"These emails were different. They weren't messages. They were photos."

"Of what?"

"Everly. Baby photos, toddler photos, birthday photos through the years, and even one of Everly in the casket at her funeral. If her mother was the one who sent them, I assume she wanted Jack to feel guilty about her daughter's death. Maybe she assumed if he did, he'd settle the case and give them the money they wanted."

Terry crossed one leg in front of the other. "How much do you know about Jack? About his personal life?"

His comment seemed to suggest there were things about Jack I may not have known, and I wondered what he was getting at.

"I've spent time with him here and there at family gatherings over the years," I said. "He was always polite, and we got along. He seemed like a good husband to my sister, and Lark adored him. I wouldn't say we had a personal relationship, though. Why do you ask?"

"Jack always acted like he had the perfect life. He'd chat with me for hours as long as the topics related to general things like which football team I wanted to win the Superbowl or what restaurants I recommended in the city. Whenever I tried to discuss topics Jack considered personal in nature, he sealed up like a vault. He'd say things were great, and that was the end of conversation."

Phoebe had always told me she'd had a close, open relationship with Jack. She said they talked about everything, but I'd never been sure how much I believed it. Jack was a pleasant, outgoing man, but I felt the same way Terry did. Jack always avoided exposing the cracks in his exterior. I could tell someone what flavor ice cream he liked or what genre of movie he preferred, but I knew nothing beyond the one-dimensional persona he presented.

"Did you know Jack hired a private investigator?" I asked.

He glanced around like he was concerned someone might eavesdrop on our conversation, even though we were the only two people in the vicinity. "I did. A few years ago, I hired a guy to find Victor, my brother. We hadn't seen each other in a couple of years, and I was worried about him."

"Why hadn't you seen him?"

"Victor prefers living off the grid. He doesn't have a job, doesn't own a cell phone, and he's always moving around. When I don't hear from him, I worry. I hired Andy Sanders to find him, and he located Victor within three days. Turned out Victor was a volunteer at a rescue zoo in Peru and had lived there for a couple of years."

Victor, it seemed, was living his best life.

"So, Jack found out about Andy Sanders through you?" I asked.

He nodded. "Jack came to my office, oh, about six weeks ago, I'd say. He asked me for the name and number of the PI I'd hired."

"Did he say why he wanted to hire him?"

Terry shook his head. "I asked, and he said he was passing Andy's information on to a friend. I wasn't sure I believed it."

"What makes you think …"

A peculiar smell wafted through the air, an earthy aroma like pine needles roasting over a campfire. I swung around and saw ashy plumes of smoke seeping through a small crack in one of the office windows.

Terry noticed it too and said, "What in the hell?"

In the distance, a male voice yelled, "Noooooooo!"

Terry and I sprinted toward the office. I arrived first and jiggled the door handle. It was locked.

"I don't understand," I said. "The office is closed now, isn't it? No one should be inside."

Terry pointed at a small, red coupe, the only other vehicle in the lot aside from ours. "That's Shane's car."

Terry fumbled in his pocket for his keys, and I pounded on the office door. "Shane! Are you in there? Can you hear me?"

There was no reply, and with every passing second, the smoke grew thicker. I whipped my phone out of my pocket and called 911. Terry slid his key into lock and opened the door.

I pushed him aside.

"Stay here," I said. "I'll handle this."

"No, you won't. It's my office. I'm going in."

"I don't have time to argue with you," I said. "Stay here. I've had training. I know what I'm doing. You don't."

It was half true.

I knew *what* to do.

I'd just never done it before.

I felt the back of the door with my hand. It was warm, but not scorching. I reached beneath my shirt and pulled my bra off. I took a bottle of water out of my handbag, poured it over my bra, and pressed it over my mouth—the best I could do with what I had.

I headed inside. The building was small, the rooms weighted with smoke. I sprinted down the hall, rounded the corner, and tried to see into the reception area. I couldn't, and my eyes burned like they'd been soaked in alcohol. But I wasn't about to back down, not until I knew Shane was safe.

I dropped onto all fours and crawled toward the reception desk. Several feet in front of me, I saw what appeared to be a shoe, and then I saw a second one. Shane was on the ground beside the desk. He appeared to be unconscious. I reached out, and my fingers slid over something sticky. I bent down lower to get a closer look and noticed the tile floor in front of me looked like I'd finger-painted it in blood.

I yanked Shane's limp body in my direction. He was heavier than I thought he'd be, and my breath grew shallower as the moments passed. Little by little, I inched him forward, but we were still several feet from the door.

A hand reached through the smoke and tugged at Shane's other leg.

I coughed a weak, "I … told … you … to … stay … outside. I … I … got this."

"Yeah, well, I've never excelled at following orders," Terry said.

Together, we managed to get Shane outside. The familiar sound of fire trucks whined in the distance—a sound I'd once found annoying was now a tune for which I would always be grateful.

I looked at Terry and said, "Thank you."

He nodded.

I eased Shane onto the ground and checked for a pulse. It was weak, but it was there. Blood seeped from the side of his head, and I noticed a two-inch gash had taken out a chunk of his hair, leaving him with an exposed skull.

I leaned down to start CPR, and the ambulance jerked to a stop beside me. Two medics jumped out and told me they'd take it from there. I backed away and stared at the nearly demolished office building in front of me.

It appeared someone had struck Shane in the side of the head, started the blaze, and left him for dead. But why?

I pressed a hand to the side of my head. It throbbed like it had been slammed into a brick wall, and I struggled to remain standing. I turned toward Terry and started to speak, but I fumbled my words. He reached out to me, and everything started spinning. Then it went black.

16

opened my eyes and looked around. I was in a hospital room, and Harvey was sitting on a chair next to me. His head was bent back like he'd nodded off. I removed the oxygen mask from my face and whispered, "Hey."

He blinked, tipped his head forward, and looked at me.

"How ya doing, kiddo?" he said.

"What happened? I remember talking to the doctor when I first arrived. I'm not sure what happened after. Did I fall asleep?"

"You were out of it when you got here." Harvey pointed to the IV bag attached to my arm. "Think they gave you something to make you feel better."

I turned.

He was right.

I'd been medicated *without* my consent.

Maybe I should have been thrilled about the happy pill they'd administered, given the hellacious evening I'd just had. But I wasn't. I didn't want to numb the pain. In the past, I'd allowed myself to suffer. I preferred to face my reality than escape it. It may have been an unhealthy way to deal with my demons and was just one of many in my arsenal of fetid vices.

I didn't care.

I'd always found people curious creatures, most choosing to flee when the first bit of wallpaper they covered themselves with peeled off long before there was a strip so big it couldn't be pasted back together again. In their haste to escape, though, they missed the important part, the lesson, the beauty that came after their insides were exposed, revealing the ugly bits, the parts they pretended didn't exist. It was easier, I supposed.

I ripped my wallpaper all the way off. I suffered. I found a twisted sense of beauty in it. A beauty those who ran from it would never see.

I yanked my IV out and tossed it to the side.

"Aww, Georgiana, come on, now," Harvey said. "Why'd ya have to go and undo what they did? They're just trying to help."

"I never told anyone it was okay to dope me up," I said.

"You're right," a male voice said. "*I* did."

Somehow in my present lethargic state, I'd failed to notice Liam leaning against the hospital door, standing in silence with his arms folded. He took one look at my expression and grinned, as if he enjoyed seeing me annoyed.

"What are you doing here, Liam?" I asked.

"The hospital called me," he said. "I'm still listed as your emergency contact."

"How can they ... why didn't you tell them we're no longer married?"

He shrugged. "I dunno. I didn't want to complicate things, I guess."

"You have the right to be consulted, not the right to make decisions on my behalf," I said. "What's wrong with the people in this place?"

I grabbed a remote control on the side of my bed and clicked it about a hundred times. Seconds later, the door opened, and Tracy Rhodes came strolling in. She took one look at me and pivoted.

"Oh, no," I said. "Don't you walk away from me. What are *you* doing here?'"

"I ... work here."

I squinted and took a hard look at the scrubs I somehow failed to notice she was wearing.

"Since when?" I said. "When I saw you last you were still working at the bar."

She moved a hand to her hip. "Yeah, well, things change. I'm a nursing aide now."

"Who stuck the IV in me when I fell asleep?"

"It was ... umm ... I mean, it was one of the other ... I can get her if you want."

"I do want. I also want to leave. Find whoever needs to discharge me or I'll discharge myself."

"All right," she said. "Let me go get someone to talk to you about it."

There was nothing to talk about.

My decision had been made.

"Let me try this another way," I said. "I'm leaving. Run along and tell whomever you need to tell."

"I mean, you can't leave without the doctor coming in and dismissing you."

"Dismissing me?"

"You know ... he needs to say it's okay for you to go."

"I think the word you want is *discharge, not dismiss*. How long have you worked here?"

"Come on," Liam said. "Lighten up. It's not her fault."

A flustered Tracy shook her head and threw her hands in the air. "It's my third day, all right? Give me a break, Georgiana!"

"Did you want that break before or after we discuss you opening your big mouth and telling my brother things that weren't your business to tell?"

Harvey ran a hand across his brow, and his face went red. "I'm not sure what's happening here, but let's button it up and save it for another time when I'm not around."

Tracy whipped around and stomped out of the room.

Liam flashed me a disappointed glance and followed her out.

"I can't believe he's chasing her, after what she did," I said.

Harvey stood and patted me on the leg. "Well, I see you haven't lost your grit, honey."

I hadn't lost my grit, but it was possible I'd lost my mind.

"I'm sorry, Harvey. I shouldn't have laid into her in front of you. It wasn't right. I'm not myself right now."

"Listen, I get it. You seem like you can take things from here, so I'm going to leave you now, and I'll see you tomorrow. I'm not telling you what to do or anything, but I'd like it if you stayed here tonight. I can look in on Luka for you. I can even bring him to the house so he's not alone tonight."

"I can't stay here. You know how I feel about hospitals."

"Yeah, I get it. Never met many people who care to spend time in hospitals, though."

"I know you're trying to look out for me, but I need to leave this place."

"All right, fine. No more police work tonight. I mean it. You go home and get some rest, and then start fresh in the morning."

He winked at me and headed for the door.

"Hey, Harvey," I said.

"Yeah?"

"You haven't said anything about Shane. How's he doing, and what room is he in? I'd like to stop in before I head out."

Harvey breathed a heavy sigh.

"I, uhh .... I meant to tell you before. You know, when he got here, he'd lost a lot of blood. The doctor did what he could, and he thought he'd be able to repair the damage. I'm sorry to say Shane didn't make it through surgery. Poor kid died about an hour ago."

17

I took Luka for a walk the next morning, made a scrambled-egg burrito to go, and dropped Luka at Aunt Laura's for the day. I checked in with Harvey, and he said the thumb print Silas had sent over had not been a match to any of the current employees at the network. Once again, we were at a stalemate.

I pulled in front of the Navarros' place just before seven. They had a small home. It was stucco and painted a shade of pink that reminded me of Pepto Bismol. A child's bike was turned over on the lawn. It was red and had a black-and-white polka-dot basket on the front. The Navarros had no other children, so I assumed the bike had been Everly's and had been rested there for some time. I sat for a moment and stared at it. I pictured her on the bike, breezing down the road with her friends. I thought about how much her parents had suffered. I had no desire to add to it, or to drive the knife deeper into their souls than it had already been driven.

On days like today, being a detective wasn't easy.

I shelved my emotions and walked to the door. I raised a fist, prepared to knock, and the door swung open. A woman leaned against it and stared at me. She had long, black hair, a slim, narrow face, and wore a loose-fitting, white, spaghetti-strap dress which was several sizes too big. She had crooked teeth, which told me her parents had been too poor to afford braces. I guessed she was in her early forties. She was a tiny speck of a thing, and it looked like she hadn't eaten anything but salad in some time.

"Lenore Navarro?" I said.

She nodded. "Who are you?"

"Detective Germaine. I'm looking into the murder of Jack Donovan and the disappearance of his daughter Lark."

She stepped back, confused. "What are you talking about?"

"A couple nights ago, Jack was shot in his back yard. He's dead."

She slapped a hand against her mouth. "Doctor Donovan is dead? Wow. I can't believe it."

Her lack of knowledge about the murder seemed odd. It had been two days since the murder and kidnapping had taken place. She should have known what had gone on, which meant she'd either missed her calling as an A-list actress or had been living in isolation. I wouldn't know which until I probed further.

"How do you not know about what happened to Jack?" I asked. "It's all over the news."

"We decided to take a break from the news after our daughter died. What we've been through is hard enough. I don't have it in me to listen to the doom and gloom of others. And that's all the news is nowadays, isn't it? It's littered with sob stories, or it's fake. Why are you here?"

"I have a few questions about your recent interactions with Jack. Can we talk?"

"No, we can't. He got what he wanted. Now leave us alone."

"I'm sure he *wanted* your daughter's operation to be a success."

She shook her head. "You misunderstand me. I'm talking about the settlement we hoped to get in court."

"What about it?"

"The judge threw it out. Said something about the paperwork we signed and us knowing the risks of the procedure. Blah, blah, blah. Bunch of crap if you ask me."

"When did this happen?" I asked.

She thought about it. "Oh, about three days back, I guess."

I studied the bike on the lawn.

For a split second, I allowed my mind to wander.

What if Everly *hadn't been* the last one on the bike?

What if the Navarros killed Jack and took his daughter because *he* had taken theirs?

My imagination had taken off and was set to sprint for the finish line.

I wanted to storm inside the house.

I wanted to throw open every door.

I wanted one of those doors to lead to Lark.

I closed my eyes and forced myself to remain in the present, to stay in a rational, open-minded state.

The bike was insignificant at the moment.

There was nothing to confirm my suspicions.

Not yet.

"You can refuse to talk to me now, or you can refuse to talk to me at the police station," I said. "Your call. Whether it's today or it's tomorrow, we will talk."

She shot me a fevered glare, like I was made of stone. "How does it feel to be a cold-hearted robot so focused on getting justice you have no sympathy for the pain of others?"

I'd been called a lot of things, but this particular insult was new.

"Excuse me?" I said.

"Do you even care about what we're going through?" She held a hand up in front of her. "Wait, don't answer. Of course, you don't. I'm just another faceless person for you to interrogate."

"Do you care about what *I'm* going through?" I asked.

She huffed a laugh. "Nothing you could be going through would ever compare to what we've just been through. What would you know about suffering?"

Plenty.

More than she'd ever know.

"Jack was my brother-in-law, and Lark is my niece," I said. "Believe me, I know."

Her eyes widened. She stared at me for a time and then dug into her dress pocket, pulled out a lighter and a cigarette, lit up, and said, "Want one?"

I shook my head. "No thanks."

"You know something? I never smoked before my daughter died. Never tried a cigarette my entire life until now. Strange the effect tragedy can have on a person."

"It's not easy," I said. "I know."

"I was standing in line at the gas station, and I saw a box of Ring Pops on the counter. They were Everly's favorite when she was alive. She used to play dress up and slide one on her ring finger and imagine she was a bride on her wedding day. That day at the gas station, I just stood there, staring at the box. I thought about my daughter and how she'd imagined a wedding day she'd never have. It was too much. I decided to leave before I lost it in front of everyone in the store, and my eyes came to rest on a pack of cigarettes."

She took a few more puffs, snuffed it out on the doorjamb, and flicked what was left of the cigarette into the grass.

"I'm sorry about what happened to your daughter," I said.

"Yeah, well, sorry won't change the way things are now. What I will say is I know nothing about what happened to the doctor. I'm sure it comes as no surprise to hear I'm apathetic toward the news of his death. I'm sorry for his daughter and his family, but we had nothing to do with it."

"After your daughter died, Jack received daily emails, each with an attached photo of Everly."

Lenore blinked at me like I'd spoken gibberish. "Why would anyone send him photos of *our* daughter?"

"The address on the emails was from a Gmail account in your name."

"I don't know what to say," she said. "I've had no correspondence with him since Everly died."

"So, you didn't vandalize his car?"

"I … what I meant was, I haven't seen him in person. My lawyer asked me not to communicate with him at all after the incident with his car, so I didn't. My lawyer wanted everything to go through him. As far as Doctor Donovan's car goes, I was angry. It may not have been the mature thing to do, but I don't regret what I did."

"And you didn't send him any emails?"

She pulled the door all the way open and waved me inside. "Come with me."

I accepted the invitation and followed her into the living room.

"Look around," she said. "What do you see?"

I canvassed the room.

I saw nothing of note.

"I'm not sure what you want me to see," I said.

"Maybe I should ask the question another way. What *don't* you see?"

I scanned the room again, this time with more scrutiny.

The furniture was out of date and looked like it had been purchased at a yard sale or second-hand store. The gray-and-white striped wallpaper was dingy and dated. The kitchen faucet had a slow leak. Someone in the house was addicted to *People* magazine, and no one in the house knew how to put their shoes away. There were photos of people I assumed were family and friends, but none of them included Everly. Aside from the bike in the yard, the inside of the house made it seem like she'd never existed.

"There are no photos of your daughter in here," I said.

"I cry when I see anything that reminds me of her," she said. "Except for the day I messed with Doctor Donovan's car, I haven't even been out of the house since the funeral."

It explained why the bike had not been moved.

"I want you to know," she said, "whoever sent those messages to Doctor Donovan, it wasn't me."

"What about your husband? Could he have sent them?"

"Manuel? No. He's not too savvy when it comes to using a computer. He doesn't send emails."

When I'd first walked inside, I'd heard voices coming from another part of the house. "Is he here?"

She nodded. "He's downstairs watching *Spenser Confidential* with my brother Franko. I'm telling you, Manuel's a gentle soul. He didn't do it. He wouldn't."

"I'd still like to talk to him."

She tapped her foot on the ground, unsure of whether she wanted to grant me access or not.

I waited.

"Manuel has been depressed since our daughter died," she said. "Each day he seems a little worse than the day before. It's hard enough to deal with my own emotions. If he keeps going downhill, I don't know what I'll do."

"I won't be long, and I'll go easy on him. I just have a few questions."

There was another lengthy pause, and then she said, "Yeah, I guess it would be all right. Wait here. I'll go get him."

She descended the stairs, and I backed up a couple feet and opened the first door in the hallway next to the kitchen. I poked my head inside and looked around. The room had been Everly's. A Disney Princess quilt rested atop an unmade bed. There were Barbie dolls scattered along the floor, and an empty potato-chip bag rested on top of a small, student-sized desk. It looked innocent and welcoming, like Everly had stepped out for a moment and would skip back into the room soon to scoop up her dolls and resume playtime. The room was alive, teeming with life, but she wasn't.

I heard movement on the stairs, and I closed the door and returned to the spot I'd stood at before.

Manuel Navarro didn't make eye contact with me when he entered the room. He shoved his hands into his pockets and stood behind Lenore like she offered a barrier of protection against me. He was a foot shorter than she was and had thick, black, unruly hair. He was dressed in faded jeans and a brown T-shirt with a giant, cartoonish-looking taco on the front. A word bubble attached to the taco's mouth said, "Let's Taco About It."

"Manuel, I'm Detective Germaine. I wanted to ask you a few questions."

He stared at the floor and nodded.

"It's no big deal, Manuel," Lenore said. "Answer her questions, and she'll go on her way."

"Manuel," I said, "were you aware Jack ... I mean Doctor Donovan, was murdered a couple of nights ago?"

He shook his head, but his hands told a different story.

They were shaking.

"Have you been sending emails to Doctor Donovan?"

"No."

"Someone lit Doctor Donovan's office on fire last night," I said. "His office assistant, Shane Curtis, is dead."

Lenore slapped a hand over her mouth. "I ... I can't believe it. Why didn't you say anything when you got here? What happened?"

"We're not sure yet."

"We may have had our issues with the doctor," Lenore said, "but Shane was one of the sweetest boys we've ever met." She elbowed Manuel's arm. "Right? Tell her how much we liked him."

Manuel's face was so flushed it looked like it was about to erupt with a downpour of emotion. He knew something I didn't, maybe something Lenore didn't know, either. If I pushed a bit more, it may have been enough to tip him over the edge.

"Manuel?" I said. "Whatever you can tell me, no matter how big or small it seems, helps. Is there anything you want to say?"

He wiped a hand across his sweaty face, looked at his wife, and said, "I'm … so … sorry, Lenore. We didn't mean for it to happen. It was an accident."

18

Y ou didn't mean for *what* to happen?" I asked.

"Manuel," Lenore said. "What is going on? Did you do something you shouldn't have?"

"I mean, I kinda did," he said.

Lenore smacked him on the side of the head. "Whatever it is, spit it out."

"What the doctor did … what he put us through … it wasn't right," Manuel said. "We lost our little girl, and then we lost the lawsuit. No one cares about us or our family or what we've gone through."

Lenore grabbed Manuel by the shoulders and shook him. "Look at me, Manuel. What did you do?"

"I mean, I didn't do anything," he said. "I just … I … I helped. I didn't know anyone was going to get hurt."

"Helped how?" I asked.

Downstairs, I heard a loud crack.

I glared at Manuel. "Who else was involved? Franko?"

Manuel lowered his head.

He seemed so frail and harmless, more of a mouse than a rat. It was hard to believe he'd done anything, even though it was clear he had.

I raced downstairs.

Lenore chased after me.

She proclaimed her brother was innocent and begged me to leave him alone.

There was no one in the basement when I got to it. A metal floor lamp had been tipped over onto the ground. The glass lampshade on top of it was broken and had chipped off a quarter-size piece of tile floor upon impact.

"Franko," I called out. "Where are you?"

There was no reply.

I turned to Lenore. "How many rooms are down here?"

"Don't jump to conclusions, Detective. You don't even know the whole story yet. I'm sure my brother can clear all of this up."

"How many rooms, Lenore?" I said. "And which one is his?"

"Two rooms." She pointed down the hall. "He's staying in the one on the right."

I barreled down the hall and looked behind door number two. It was empty, but the window was open, and the screen had been yanked from the frame and tossed onto the bed.

Franko was gone.

19

called for backup and told Lenore and Manuel to remain inside the house while I surveyed the neighborhood. The street was wide and littered with houses. Franko could have been anywhere. I slid inside the Jeep and drove down the road, hoping I'd catch sight of him. For several minutes, I saw nothing of note. Then I got lucky. A man I assumed was Franko, dressed in a neon-yellow shirt, bright enough to see on the foggiest of days, made the mistake of exiting through the front gate of a yard at the end the Navarros' street. He turned toward the Jeep, saw me see him, and ran down the middle of the street in the opposite direction—a rookie mistake.

I assessed my options.

Option one.

Pull over and chase him.

Option two.

Slow him down by shooting him in the leg.

Option one was less desirable, and option two was careless on several levels, including the fact I was in a populated neighborhood.

I exercised a third option and decided a love tap was in order. Not a big one. I didn't want to cause serious injury. I just wanted to stop him. I pressed on the gas pedal until the front of the Jeep caught up with him and then tapped him in the buttocks. He launched a few feet into the air and came down on his chest.

Ouch.

The tap had been a bit more forceful than I'd expected. Still, it achieved the desired effect. I threw the door open, exited the Jeep, and walked over to him. He turned toward me and yelled something in Spanish. I didn't know Spanish. I did know whatever he'd just called me, *muchacha loca,* couldn't have been polite.

"Are you Franko?"

He didn't respond.

"You can answer me, or this can get worse," I said. "Up to you."

His defiant eyes showed little concern for his own welfare, but I knew he cared. Everyone *always* did. I lifted my shirt enough for him to see my hand resting on my gun.

"Doctor Donovan was my brother-in-law," I said. "He's dead. Someone killed him the other night and then abducted my niece. You know what I think? I think there's a chance that someone was you. You can either tell me where she is, right here, right now, or I'll end your life."

"I didn't do it!" he said. "It wasn't me."

"You are Franko, though, correct? You're Lenore's brother?"

"I am."

It was a start.

I told myself I wouldn't have shot him.

I was a better person than that, a better detective.

I was fair, and I was just.

But if his demeanor had indicated he'd taken Lark, I wasn't certain what I would have done. I bent down to scoop Franko and his injured derriere off the ground so I could zip-tie his wrists. At that moment, Harvey rolled by me so slow I could see the shocked expression on his face as he assessed the scene and realized what he thought I'd done. I'd known him for so long I assumed nothing I did would shock him.

I was wrong.

He pressed a hand to his forehead and mouthed something like, "*Oh, no. She didn't. She wouldn't.*"

But I had done it, and given the same situation, I'd do it again, even though I knew there'd be hell to pay.

20

Lenore, Manuel, and Franko were taken to the police station and put into separate rooms. Manuel and Franko were questioned first. Afterward, I was convinced they hadn't taken Lark, and they hadn't murdered Jack. Manuel and Franko may have been idiots, and they may have been guilty of arson and the murder of Shane Curtis, but they had no information about Lark's whereabouts.

The interrogation revealed days earlier Lenore and Manuel had received a call from their lawyer. Their lawyer had spoken with Jack's lawyer, and he was almost certain Jack would be found innocent of any wrongdoing in their daughter's death. The Navarros' lawyer agreed, which meant there would be no reckoning for Jack, and there would be no payout. A day after the devastating news, Franko came to town. He filled Manuel's ear with ideas of revenge, a way to get back at Jack without going through court. A plan was hatched to teach Jack a lesson he'd never forget. No one would get hurt, and no one did at first, until their plan fell apart.

The night before, Manuel and Franko had parked their car across the street and waited for Shane to leave the office. Shane locked up a few minutes after five and drove out of the parking lot. Then amateur hour began.

Manuel and Franko walked behind the office, busted a window, and climbed through it. Before they had the chance to torch the place, the front door to the office opened, and Shane walked in. He'd forgotten his cell phone. Shane reached for it, saw Manuel and Franko, and froze.

Shane offered to take his cell phone and go, no questions asked, but a paranoid Franko grabbed a crystal paperweight off the desk and bashed Shane on the side of the head. Shane fell to the ground. When the reality of what had just happened set in, Manuel decided to abort the mission. He suggested they place an anonymous call to the police using the office phone and get out of there. At first, Franko appeared keen to go along with the plan. Manuel slipped back out the window and looked back, expecting Franko to be in tow. What he saw instead was Franko light a match and hold it over the office curtains.

Manuel yelled, "Nooooo," which Terry and I had heard.

But it was already too late.

Distraught, Manuel decided once he got home, he'd call the police and turn himself in. Then Franko had said, "Lenore has been through enough. She just lost her daughter. What do you think will happen if she loses you too?"

He didn't know what she'd do. But thinking about it had been enough to keep him quiet until now. I wanted to believe Manuel would have done the right thing in the end. I wanted to believe he would have confessed. Maybe I gave him the benefit of the doubt because he'd been through so much already.

I didn't know.

What I did know now was who sent the emails to Jack from Lenore's account. Firestarter Franko.

It was Lenore's turn. I entered the room where she had been waiting and explained the details we'd learned from her husband and brother. She didn't want to believe it, even though she did.

"Manuel and Franko both said you knew nothing about their plan to burn Doctor Donovan's office down or what had happened when they did," I said.

"I didn't know," she said. "If I would have, I would have stopped them. Even if Shane hadn't been there, I wouldn't have wanted them to take it as far as they did."

"You went a bit far when you vandalized Jack's car."

"I know. It was stupid. And now I can't help but wonder if what I did led to what they did last night."

"You may have started it, but they made their own choices, and I imagine they left you out of the loop because they knew what you'd say."

She stared at the table and frowned. "What will happen to them?"

"They're being booked for arson and felony murder. Your brother initiated it all, so odds are he'll face more prison time. Hard to say until it goes to trial."

She pressed her face into her hands and sobbed. "What do I do now? I've lost everything."

"I know what you've been through is rough," I said, "but there is life after this, even after all you've faced. I wouldn't say it if I didn't know it was true."

"How could there be? I have nothing left to live for anymore. I have nothing and no one."

Right now, she needed someone on her side, someone willing to fight for her.

"Hang tight for a minute," I said. "I'll be right back."

I walked to my office and grabbed a business card out of my

desk drawer. I had no intention of helping Franko. He needed to pay for what he'd done and do his time for the life he took. But Manuel didn't deserve to share his fate.

I returned to the interrogation room, held the card out to Lenore, and said, "Here's the name of someone who can help."

Lenore wiped her tears on her sweater, took the card, and stared at it. "Tiffany Wheeler. Who's she?"

"An attorney. A good attorney."

"I already have an attorney."

"This isn't a lawsuit. You need a criminal defense lawyer. Tiffany's the best I've seen. She's tough, and she's fair. She's who I would call if I were in your position."

She pushed the card into her back pocket. "I love my brother, and I don't want to see anything happen to him, but I could kill him for what he's done."

"I understand his motivation. He was in pain because you were in pain. He just shouldn't have acted on his impulses."

"I can't even ... it's all a ... I need a cigarette."

"Have one. You're free to go."

"Can I see Manuel first?"

"I can ask," I said.

"Would you?"

I nodded and started for the door.

"Hey," she said.

I glanced back. "Yeah?"

"Why are you helping me?"

I supposed I'd offered Tiffany's card because I felt Lenore and I were connected on an empathetic level—one she couldn't see and didn't know about. There was a time when my emotions had mirrored her own. Today I'd questioned her while trying not to get swept up in problems that weren't mine. But I had. I could feel it, the tense uneasiness fraying the marrow in my bones.

"I'm just doing my job," I said.

"You're not, though. You didn't have to recommend a lawyer to me. Why did you?"

"I'm sorry for what you've gone through and for what's happening now. You deserve a fresh start in life."

21

A couple of hours later, I was on my way out of the police station, and Harvey stopped me.

"I've been looking for you," he said.

"Why?" I asked.

"Wheeler is in your office. He wants to talk to you."

Whatever Wheeler wanted, I assumed it wasn't good.

"How about I slip out, and you tell him I left before you had the chance to tell me he wanted to see me?"

"He'd just ask me where you're staying and show up at your place. Better here than there, right?"

"How much does he know about what happened earlier today?"

"Everything, I'd say. Franko Sanchez called his lawyer after his sister refused to let him use theirs, and his lawyer called Wheeler."

"Of course, he did."

There were few things I fancied less in life than a conversation with Wheeler. We had history, and it wasn't good. The first time we met I was a pint-sized ten-year-old. He was my elementary school teacher. He didn't like me then, and he didn't like me now.

Wheeler's overall disdain for me began when his daughter, Tiffany, decided it was a good idea to steal a snack-size bag of Cheetos out of my A-Team lunchbox. I'd walked away to buy a carton of chocolate milk, and Tiffany seized the opportunity. She pinched my bag of chips and speed-walked away.

I returned to the table, went to grab the chips, and realized they'd been taken. I slammed my lunchbox shut, crossed my arms, and glared at the potential offenders around me. Worried I'd place the blame on them, the two boys on the bench across from me raised their fingers in unison and gave up Tiffany and her location.

Terrified, Tiffany shoved the chips beneath the elastic waistband on her skirt and made a run for it. The chips broke free soon after she took off. I could have snatched them up, returned to the table, and forgotten all about it.

I *could* have.

But I didn't.

In that moment, I no longer cared about the chips I'd lost. She'd attempted to savor a snack that wasn't hers. If she got away with it, others may have followed suit, and I decided she needed to be taught a lesson.

I caught up to Tiffany, made a fist, and swung, unaware of how much pack there was to my punch. Blood sprayed out of her nose and soiled the perfect pastel dress she was wearing. She looked down and screamed because she looked like she'd come straight off the set of Stephen King's *Carrie*. To make matters worse, I'd broken her nose. From that day on, the kids at school called her Squirt, a name some still used to refer to her, even though we were all adults. Wheeler found out what happened to his daughter and transferred me out of his class. He told the principal he needed to keep me away from him because he worried about what he'd do to me if he saw me.

Such a grownup.

Tiffany and I didn't speak to each other for years. In our junior year of high school, I walked by the bleachers next to the football field and heard someone crying. I ducked beneath them and found Tiffany sitting on the ground with her head buried in her knees. An empty bottle of tequila was turned on its side next to her. The bits and pieces of coherent information she slurred in my direction let me know her boyfriend had dumped her that day because she refused to put out, and he was tired of waiting. The alcohol had been supplied from her friend Nina, who'd stolen it out of her parents' cupboard when she went home for lunch. Nina left the bottle with Tiffany and trotted off to class, leaving Tiffany to fend for herself.

I stayed with Tiffany for the rest of the day. When school got out, she still wasn't sober, and she was apprehensive over the thought of going home. She was tormented over what her father might do if he found out about the tequila. So, I took her to my house, smuggled her into my room, and Paul helped me clean her up. I had her call her mother and say we were working on an assignment for school. By the time her nine o'clock curfew rolled around, I'd fed her a gallon of water, redressed her in some of my clothes, fixed her hair, and driven her home with strict instructions to say hello to her parents when she walked in, yawn like she was tired, and then head straight to bed. My plan worked, and from then on, we were friends.

Tiffany forgave me for my crime of passion, but her father never did, which made the face-to-face we were about to have all the more awkward.

I walked into my office and closed the door. Wheeler was sitting in my chair with his hands clasped over his sizable belly. He had even less hair on his head than the last time I'd seen him and about twice the wrinkles.

What a difference a couple of years made.

"You wanted to see me," I said.

He cleared his throat and made a humming sound like he was prepping the speech he'd rehearsed. "Did you or did you not run a man down with your vehicle today?"

"I wouldn't say I *ran him down*. The guy took off when he saw me. He made the choice to sprint down the middle of the street. It seemed like a good opportunity to catch him, so I acted on it."

"You *acted* on it."

"Yeah. I caught up to him and gave him a little nudge, you know, just to get him to pump the brakes."

"A *nudge*? His lawyer has threatened to sue."

"Franko whatever-his-last-name-is—"

"Sanchez."

"Sanchez chose to take off rather than answer my questions," I said. "He's also guilty of murder."

"It doesn't matter. You can't run people down with your vehicle, Georgiana!"

"So, it's okay for him to kill Shane Curtis and burn Jack's office building to the ground, but I can't do what I need to do to apprehend the guy? He's fine. He didn't get hurt much, and *he's* still alive. He should feel lucky he didn't get hit harder."

"His arm is broken, and so is his tailbone."

An arm and a tailbone.

Didn't seem like a big deal to me.

"He'll heal," I said.

Wheeler huffed a disgusted sigh. "I knew there'd be trouble when Harvey told me you'd come back. Hasn't even been a week yet, and you're already causing problems."

"I'm doing what needs to be done for Jack and Lark."

He stood up and scooped his jacket off my desk. "I hear you gave Tiffany's business card to Lenore Navarro."

I nodded. "You heard right."

"I don't want her working their case."

"It doesn't matter what *you* want. Tiffany will decide for herself. She's free to choose which cases she takes and which she doesn't. Franko Sanchez may be an enabling dirtbag, but the Navarros are good people who deserve good representation."

He grunted something under his breath. "About what happened today ... I don't have time to come down here and scold you every time you go off the rails."

I shrugged. "Don't, then."

He pointed at me and said, "Keep it up and you'll be off this case."

He looked like he wanted to string me up. I may have been forty-two, but when he looked at me, he still saw a smug, entitled cop's kid. He may have ascended to a higher position in life, but it didn't mean he hadn't gotten a heap of dirt on himself along the way. Dirt I happened to know about.

"It's not a good idea to threaten me," I said. "You know it isn't."

He caught my meaning, opened the office door, and we locked eyes. For a moment, it seemed he'd flashed back to an old memory, one he wasn't proud of—and one he couldn't change.

No matter who we were or where we came from, we were all scarred.

Him.

Me.

All of us had battle wounds, dark stains which offered reminders of moments in time when we could have been our best selves, but we weren't. I had no desire to raise his to the surface again, as long as he didn't stand between me and what it took to find Lark.

22

ark had been missing for almost seventy-two hours, and I was no closer to finding her. She felt far away, out of my reach. Up to now, I had chased dead ends. I needed to find a live one.

Hattie had built the first house in Jack and Phoebe's neighborhood and knew all the residents by name. She was the kind of woman I imagined slept with a pair of binoculars beneath her pillow at night, because every time I'd visited my sister in the past, Hattie had more than her fair share of gossip to discuss about the residents in her suburb.

I walked to Hattie's door, pulled the screen door open, and was about to knock when the main door creaked open on its own. I stuck my head inside.

"Hattie, you here? It's Georgiana, Phoebe's sister."

There was no response.

I stood for a moment and listened.

It was quiet.

Too quiet.

I readied my gun and showed myself inside, heading down the hallway after I'd heard movement in the kitchen. I rounded the corner and found Hattie bent over the stove, stirring whatever she was cooking. I tapped her on the shoulder. She whipped around, blinked at the gun in my hand, and dropped the wooden spoon she'd been holding.

"What are you trying to do, give me a heart attack?" she said.

Oops.

My bad.

I backed up and holstered the gun.

"Sorry," I said. "Your front door opened on its own. I called out to you, and you didn't answer."

She tapped her foot on the floor. "I wasn't expecting anyone. I don't have my hearing aids in. As for the door, it's been giving me problems for a while now. It doesn't shut the way it's supposed to anymore. Sometimes I lock the screen. Other times I don't. Depends on what I'm doing."

"You need to get your door looked at."

"No, I don't. Seems like a great big hassle if you ask me. I'd call someone to come out. He'd show up, see I'm getting up there in years, and give me a ridiculous bid about five times more than he'd give one of my neighbors. No siree."

"It isn't safe to have an unlocked door after what just happened."

She opened a kitchen drawer, reached in, and pulled out a spectacular specimen of a thing. She pointed it at me like she intended to use it, and I hopped back.

"Sheesh," she said. "I'm not trying to stab ya. I'm trying to show you the artistry on this knife."

I leaned in.

"This is a Tsukasa White Steel Enryu Kurouchi Damascus Wa-Gyuto," she said.

"A ... what?"

"It's Japanese. It was given to my late husband when he visited Japan." She flattened it in her hands. "See the knife's design? It's hand-forged using carbon steel and then twisted, giving it a Damascus pattern. Takes more than six months to make. One stab to the abdomen with this beauty, and any intruder who dares step foot inside my house won't live to see another day."

She stared at the knife in awe, like she welcomed the opportunity to use it one day for something other than cooking. Although the knife was the most impressive piece of cutlery I'd ever seen, unless she was quicker on the draw, an intruder could get to her before she got to him.

"I can ask Harvey to take a look at the door when he gets a chance," I said. "If it's an easy fix, I'd guess he wouldn't charge you anything."

She shrugged. "If you must. Like I said, I'm not worried. Been wondering what's taken you so long to come here, and why you haven't stopped by sooner. Thought you'd come over when you first got back into town."

"I've been busy. I've had a lot of leads to follow up on."

"Any of them get you closer to the deviant who took Lark?"

I shook my head. "Not yet."

She placed the knife back into the drawer and grabbed the kettle. She set it under the tap, filled it with water, and switched it on. I sat down.

"What will it be, then?" she asked.

"I want to talk about the night Lark went missing."

"I meant, what kind of tea do you fancy, dear?"

"Oh, you can choose for me. Whatever you have is fine."

She stared at me for a moment. "Hmm … you look like a girl who drinks Earl Grey or maybe even Lady Grey."

I had no idea what criteria she used to make her assessment, but I smiled and nodded anyway.

The tea boiled, and she poured us both a cup. She set mine in front of me and joined me at the table. I was about to ask her about the night Jack died when something furry rubbed against my leg.

I looked down. "Willy?"

Hattie nodded. "Phoebe asked me to keep Lark's cat for now. I don't mind. He's no bother. It's just that every time I open the front door, he bolts for it like he's trying to get out. It's not like him, you know. Up to now, I've always found him to be a rather lazy cat. I suppose he's been riled up since the other night and just wants to go home. Can't blame him. Anyhoo, what would you like to know?"

Everything.

I wanted to know everything.

All of it.

Every last detail.

"Can you tell me what happened the other night?" I asked.

"I can. It would be a repeat of what I've said to everyone else who's been here before you, though, and I'm sure they've filled you in."

"Telling me isn't the same as telling them."

"Why wouldn't it be?"

For whatever reason, it seemed Hattie was playing hard to get today.

"What did the man look like—the one you saw?" I asked.

"It was dark outside."

"I know. There are streetlamps. Try to remember."

She tapped her finger on the side of her cup. "I don't know. I guess I'd say he was average."

"You know, Hattie, I've always enjoyed our talks in the past. You have a great eye for detail. Are you sure you don't remember anything more?"

"He sprinted by the window so fast. He was in a hurry."

It may have happened the way she said it had. Still, I felt she was holding back.

"And you didn't see Lark before or after you saw the man?" I asked.

"No. I mean, I don't think so. Right before he ran by, I could have sworn I saw something shiny. I thought it was a reflection, or my mind playing tricks on me. Now I'm not so sure."

"Where did you see it?"

"In the air. I know how it sounds, but I don't know how else to explain it."

I sipped my tea and thought of ways to inspire her to talk about whatever she hadn't yet. "Lark's been gone for three days."

Hattie stared into her tea and frowned. "I know. I think about her every hour of every day."

"When a child goes missing, the first few days are crucial."

"I know."

"Do you? Almost three-quarters of people who go missing are found within twenty-four hours. After the third day, the leads tend to slow down and there's a risk the trail will go cold. I tell myself Lark's out there somewhere, alive, because I need to believe she is. But each day that passes, odds are … she isn't. I know how much you care about her. So, I'll ask one more time. If there's anything you haven't said, *now* is the time to say it."

Hattie poured some cream into her tea, swirled it around with a spoon, took a sip, and set it down. She leaned back and sighed, but she still wasn't talking.

Come on, Hattie.

Whatever it is, speak.

"There is one thing," she said. "It's not a big thing, and it will prove to be nothing more than my eyesight playing tricks on me like it does from time to time. If I tell you, I want you to promise not to go off half-cocked afterward. I know how you are at times. You rule yourself by the heart first and the head second."

She was wrong.

My heart had never been a match for my head.

"I got it," I said. "What is it?"

"The man I saw … he turned toward me for a moment when he passed. Just for a second, maybe two. I've thought about it ever since. There was something about him. Something familiar."

"You know who he reminds you of, Hattie," I said. "Name him."

"It was his physique, you know, the way he leaned forward when he ran. It reminded me of Mitch Porter."

23

Mitch Porter had been over at Jack's house the night of the murder, along with his wife Holly. I'd never heard Phoebe speak in a negative way about him, but Holly was another story. Phoebe seemed bothered by her, and I didn't understand why. I wasn't even sure Phoebe knew why. She often made assumptions about people with little evidence to back it up.

Holly had gone out of her way to become friends with Phoebe when they first moved in, after Jack and Mitch golfed together on the weekends. Holly wanted the twosome to become a foursome and suggested they all take a trip to Florida together. Everyone was on board with the idea except Phoebe, who shot it down. At the time, I'd asked her why, and she'd said she didn't know Holly well enough to commit to a five-day vacation together. I mentioned the trip seemed like the perfect time to get better acquainted. She then said she didn't trust Holly, and she changed the subject. I hadn't thought much about it since—until now.

Why didn't she trust her?

On my way out of Hattie's house, Willy remained by my side. I assumed he was planning to escape when the door opened, and I welcomed it. I wanted to see where he'd go. I opened the door, and he bolted outside. An irked Hattie threw her arms up, and I told her not to worry—I'd go after him. She shook her head and disappeared into the next room.

Willy raced in the direction of Phoebe's house. When I caught up with him, he was scratching at the door to get inside. I worried he expected to see Jack, Phoebe, and Lark on the other side of the door and what would happen when he didn't, but he ran toward Lark's room the first chance he got.

I went after him. "She's not there, Willy."

I'd said the words like I expected the cat to understand me.

Willy ignored the fact I was talking to him and kept going.

He reached Lark's room and used his nose to push the door open. I thought he might search for Lark or jump onto her bed, expecting her to be buried beneath the covers. He didn't. He stepped into his cat bed and started digging at the fabric.

"Willy," I said. "What in the world are you doing?"

He stared up at me like he thought I was an imbecile and then went back to digging. I reached down and tried to lift him up. He hissed at me, something he'd never done before, and I backed off. He knew what he wanted to do, and I needed to let him do it.

I bent down next to him and maintained my distance while I attempted to understand his strange behavior. Hunched over, I saw what I hadn't seen before—a hole in the lining of his cat bed. He wasn't digging. He was sticking his paw into the hole and pulling it out.

I tried talking to him again, this time with a calmer tone.

"What are you looking for, Willy? Can I help?"

I eased my hand toward the hole. Willy turned toward me. I waited for him to lash out and express his aggression again. He looked at me, and then at the hole, and he moved to the side. I stuck my hand into the hole, ripping a generous piece of the fabric in the process. I clawed around with my fingers for a few seconds and pulled out a ball of batting. I set it down and stared at it. Whatever the operation was, it had not been a success so far.

"I'm not sure what you're trying to do here, Willy," I said. "But I'm not going to sit here all night and pull your bed apart. Come on, I'll take you to see Phoebe. Maybe it will help."

He didn't budge.

Maybe if I took the bed with me, he'd be more inclined to follow.

I scooped him out of the bed, picked it up, and felt something hard beneath my fingers. There *was* something inside the lining of the bed. Instead of doing any further excavation, I shoved my hands inside the torn fabric and ripped the edge of the bed apart. A small, rectangular piece of metal fell out, clanking on the floor between my feet. I grabbed a tissue from a box sitting on Lark's nightstand, leaned over, and picked the metal up.

Could it have been the shiny object Hattie had seen?

I turned it over in my hand and recognized what it was—a money clip. Inscribed on one of the sides were the words *To TP with love.*

TP.

I *knew* someone with those initials.

Dr. Terry Pearson.

24

Terry was sitting on a chair on his front porch when I arrived, staring up at a sky full of stars and indulging in a beer. I parked the Jeep, and he stood up and walked over to me.

"It's a bit late for a visit," he said. "What brings you here, Detective?"

I pulled a plastic baggie out of my pocket and shoved it in front of his face. "Recognize *this*?"

He scratched his head and leaned in. "I mean, it's a bit dark out here for me to see what you're trying to show me."

"Take a closer look."

He did and then said, "You came all the way here to show me a piece of metal inside of a plastic bag? I still don't know what you're getting at. Why don't you just tell me why you're so worked up?"

A young boy no older than six with a pale-blue bathrobe wrapped around his body tiptoed onto the porch and said, "Dad? What are you doing? Who's she?"

"Don't worry about it," Terry said. "Get your pajamas on and brush your teeth. I'll tuck you in once I'm done here. Shouldn't be too long."

"You didn't tell me you had kids," I said.

"You didn't ask. I have a wife too, if you're interested. She's at the grocery store right now, but if you stick around, she'll be home soon, and then you can interrogate both of us at the same time."

His sarcasm hit hard, and I was beginning to see how the "heart before head" assessment Hattie had made about me earlier made sense. Terry didn't fit the profile of a ruthless killer who murdered his business partner and friend and then stole his child. If I'd taken a few minutes to think it through before I'd speed-raced over to his house, I wouldn't have been here now, making a fool of myself.

"I'm sorry I bothered you," I said. "I'll let you get back to your kid."

"*Kids*. We have three. Two boys and a girl. I could get them out here, and you could do a lineup of all of us to decide who is innocent and who is guilty. I mean, my son threw a few pieces of spaghetti at my daughter tonight. Hit her in the face. Made her cry. Maybe jail time is just what he needs."

Who knew the good doctor had so much grit to him? He'd struck me as a bit of a nerd when we'd first met, but now he seemed to be the complete opposite. His attempt to belittle me had been a success. My wound was salted to capacity.

"I … I just … I shouldn't have …"

"You're right," he said. "You shouldn't have. I don't appreciate being accused without having a chance to respond first. I'm guessing whatever you found relates to me in some way, or you think it does, at least. Right?"

"I thought it did. I don't anymore. It was all a mistake."

"A mistake? I risked my life for you yesterday. The least you could have done was give me the benefit of the doubt."

I couldn't imagine taking the time to explain myself would have made things any better, but I decided to try. "I found something tonight at Jack and Phoebe's house."

"I assume whatever you found is in the plastic bag."

I nodded.

"Let's go in the house so I can get a better look at it," he said.

"It's okay. It's not necessary. I'm sorry I bothered you."

"It's *not* okay. What is it?"

"A money clip."

"What does a money clip have to do with me?"

"It … uhh … has your initials on it along with the inscription '*with love.*'"

He nodded. "I see. Well, I've never carried a money clip. I'm a wallet kind of guy."

He dug inside his pocket, pulled his wallet out, and waved it in front of me. He was right.

I flashed back to a memory from the evening before when Terry and I met in the parking lot outside the office. He'd left his wallet on the dashboard when he stepped out of his truck to talk to me. It didn't mean he didn't own or carry a money clip, but I now felt certain he wasn't the man I was after.

"And if you met my wife," he continued, "you'd know she'd *never* give me a keepsake inscribed 'with love.' She's a good woman. She's just not a sentimental one. Last year I received a subscription to *Classic Motoring* magazine for my birthday. The year before, she gave me the same thing. The year before, the same. I've received the same magazine subscription five years in a row now."

The broad's not sappy.

I get it.

"I'm going to leave now," I said.

"Hang on," he said. "Where did you find the money clip? I

thought the police would have combed the entire house and collected everything as evidence."

Hunter had helped with combing the house, and I was sure she'd done her best. A cat bed wasn't an obvious place to look. "I didn't find the money clip."

"What do you mean?"

"Lark's cat Willy did. I don't know where he found it, but he dragged it back to a hidey-hole he had in his bed."

He shrugged. "Makes a bit more sense to me now."

"What does?"

"Jack once told me their cat liked to bring them trinkets he found outside when he wandered around the neighborhood."

"Did he say anything else about it?"

He shook his head, turned, and headed for the door.

"You should ask Phoebe," he said. "I'm sure she'd know."

25

felt like I'd lost my sense of self, the part of me that discerned right from wrong and good choices over bad ones. To find Lark, I needed to think smarter, be smarter, keep my heart out of my head. I needed to resist pouncing on clues without giving enough thought to their legitimacy. I didn't want to admit it, but I was tainted. The investigation was personal, and if I kept going the way I had been, it would lead to an infinite number of screwups.

I considered calling Hunter to ask if she could follow up on a couple of leads for me and taking time the next day to clear my head. I even took out my cell phone and stared at the screen for a while. Then I pocketed it. I couldn't allow her to take over, not even for a second. I may not have been in the perfect headspace, but I'd owned where I'd failed, and I told myself realization was the key to turning it all around.

Wasn't it?

Tomorrow was a new day.

A fresh day.

Tomorrow, the answers would come.

Tomorrow, I would find Lark.

I draped an arm around Luka and leaned back on the pillow. I thought about my plans for the next day, where I would go, whom I would interrogate. I filtered all of the unanswered questions I still had through my mind.

Could Mitch Porter have been the man Hattie saw out her window?

Why didn't Phoebe like his wife?

Who was Phoebe's stalker?

And why did Jack hire a private investigator right before he died?

My cell phone rang. I viewed the time. It was half past nine at night, and Harvey was on the line. I guessed he wanted an update. Or maybe Terry Pearson had called to complain about being accused of crimes he didn't commit. Either way, I didn't feel like talking. I sent Harvey a text and said I needed rest and that I'd come see him in the morning.

I had peopled enough for one day.

I was all peopled out.

My phone rang again ten minutes later, and I realized my former assumption could have been wrong. Maybe Harvey hadn't called to get an update. Maybe he'd called to give me one instead.

I decided to find out, answering the call without even looking at the screen.

"Hey, Harvey," I said. "It's late. Is everything all right?"

"Georgiana?" a man's voice said.

The man's tone was smoky and deep.

It *wasn't* Harvey.

"Who is this?" I asked.

"It's Giovanni. Giovanni Luciana."

"Gio? It's … I can't believe—"

"I'm sorry. I didn't mean to call this late. I've been out of town. I just returned, and my uncle gave me your message. I can reach out another time if you prefer."

I *didn't* prefer.

In the few seconds I'd listened to him talk, my body had relaxed. My shoulders no longer felt stiff and immotile. The sound of his voice was what I needed right now.

"It's fine," I said. "I'm glad you called. I can talk."

"How are you?"

I paused, unsure of how I wanted to answer the question and how much detail was too much detail after years of not connecting with someone.

"It's been a long day," I said. "A long *few* days. So much has happened, I don't know where to begin."

"Why don't you start at the beginning? What have you been doing since I saw you last? Where are you now? I want to know everything."

Everything could wait. For now, I decided to approach the conversation with baby steps. "I'm in Cambria. Been here off and on since I left college."

"You moved back home, then. I thought you might."

"After graduation, I returned home for a couple of months, and then I was going to take a year off and travel the world with Tiffany, a friend of mine from high school. It didn't work out."

"Why not? What happened?"

"Right before we were set to go, Tiffany found out she was accepted into the law school program at Stanford University. She suggested we do a shorter version of the trip than we'd planned, but I knew she was anxious about all the things she needed to do before she devoted her life to school for the next several years, so I gave her a pass. It was worth it. She's a hotshot lawyer in Los Angeles now."

"You should have called me. I would have traveled with you."

His comment was an unexpected one.

He couldn't have gone with me.

At the time, he was involved with someone else.

"What about you?" I said. "Are you still with Jodie?"

It was a blatant, obvious attempt to assess who was in his life and who wasn't. I didn't care. I wanted to know.

"Jodie and I broke up the day you left for home," he said. "Don't you remember?"

"I don't. You never told me the two of you broke up."

"I wrote you a letter. I left it on top of one of the boxes in your room."

"I don't know what to say except I never got it."

And I had a good idea why.

It had been intercepted.

There were times when I lived with Daniela when I could tell she didn't like to share me with her brother. She'd narrow her eyes at us, cross her arms, and sulk when she wasn't getting all of the attention. Giovanni never seemed to notice. Or maybe he had, and he hadn't thought it warranted recognition. Right before I moved home, Daniela tried to convince me to stay in New York with her. As much as I loved being there for college, New York was big enough to swallow me whole. It was her dream. It wasn't mine. Still, she had no right to do what I assumed she'd done. Her one selfish act changed everything.

"How is Daniela?" I asked.

"She runs the family business now. It suits her. I've retired from it all. Far better for her to be in charge."

Giovanni had never given me a clear answer on what the family business was all about. Whenever I'd asked, and I had a few times when we were young, Giovanni and Daniela became a united front. They'd said their father was involved in construction and dabbled in business on Wall Street. Something about the way they responded furthered my curiosity. I wanted to know. I just got the impression I was better off not knowing.

"The other day, I was thinking about the restaurant you wanted to open," I said. "Remember?"

"And yet you've never stopped by."

I was taken aback. Had he opened it after all?

"You opened Osteria dei Mascalzoni?" I said.

"I did. You should come in next time you're in New York. Let me know when you do, and I'll join you."

"All right, I will."

He paused. "It's good to talk to you. But you sound, I don't know ... There's a hint of sadness in your voice. You said the last few days had been long. Care to talk about it?"

Even after all this time, he still seemed to know me better than almost everyone else.

"I don't want to burden you with my problems on our first call together," I said.

"You could never be a burden. What is it? What's wrong?"

I closed my eyes.

I took a deep breath.

I told myself to save it for another day.

And then it all came tumbling out.

"A few days ago, when my sister was out of town for the night, her husband was murdered in their back yard, and my niece, Lark, was taken," I said. "We have no idea where she is. Every lead has led somewhere. They just haven't led to Lark or my brother-in-law's killer. Time is slipping away from me. *My niece* is slipping away from me. I'm running out of time."

"What about the police? What are they doing?"

"I'm ... ahh ... I guess you could say *I'm* the police. I'm a detective now."

"A detective? It suits you."

"I keep making mistakes. If I don't get on the right path soon, I worry I'll never find her."

"Better a diamond with a flaw than a pebble without one."

"What?"

"It's a Chinese proverb."

Of course. I remembered now. He had quoted random proverbs all the time when we were in school. I'd always assumed it was to get a rise out of his sister Daniela, who found them annoying.

"I'm a lot more pebble than diamond right now," I said.

"No, you're not. Diamonds are rare. Pebbles are common. Don't seek perfection. Don't focus on your weaknesses. Use your weaknesses to make you strong. Even when a diamond has a flaw, it's far more valuable than an unblemished pebble."

Giovanni knew the *old* Georgiana.

What would he think of the woman I was today?

"Can I do anything to help with the investigation?" he asked. "Or to help you?"

"Talking to me is helping."

More than he knew.

Over the next half hour, we filled each other in on our lives.

Giovanni had married a woman named Valentina, not because he loved her, but because his father and her father pushed them together. Giovanni's father died, and he took over the family business. Valentina bore a son. His name was Marcelo. He was eight. He wasn't Giovanni's biological son, but Giovanni was the only father the boy had ever known. Two years earlier, there had been a fire at his home. He didn't explain how it started. He just said he wasn't there when it happened. Marcelo made it out unscathed, but Valentina was trapped beneath a beam inside the house. She didn't survive. After the fire, Giovanni reassessed his life and what mattered most to him, and he handed the keys to the family's kingdom to Daniela with a promise to be there if she needed him. So far, she'd managed just fine on her own.

My turn.

I told Giovanni I'd left Cambria a few years after we graduated college and traveled on my own. I bought an RV and visited all fifty states, spending a month in each one. Living on my own, I'd realized how much I liked my autonomy. I liked who I was when I was free of the pressure that so often accompanied pleasing everyone else. After touring the States, I returned home and rekindled an old flame with a boy I'd dated in high school. I became a cop. Then a detective. I married the old flame. The marriage lasted several years and then fizzled out. I blamed myself. My life had been through its share of ups and downs, but I'd managed to find a sense of peace within the chaos.

Then Lark went missing.

Hearing myself summarize almost twenty years out loud, it seemed my life had shifted and folded until the sum of its parts had fit inside a bland, medium-size cardboard box. The box wasn't as vanilla as it appeared in the story I had just told him, though. The box had secrets of its own, and I was sure Giovanni's did too.

I wanted to stay awake and talk to him for the rest of the night. I thought I could push through and then start the day with a Red Bull and a guarana tablet, but it was almost midnight and way past my bedtime. If I was to be a diamond instead of a pebble, the diamond needed sleep.

I yawned.

"You're tired," he said. "It's late. I'll let you go. Let me know when we can speak again."

It would have been easy to return the sentiment and end the call.

But I had a knack for making things hard.

"I should have asked Daniela if you married Jodie all those years ago," I said. "I shouldn't have assumed you did."

"And I should have called you to make sure you received my letter. You were a good friend to me, Georgiana. I'm sorry I wasn't here for you over the years when you needed me. I'm here now. If you need anything, call me anytime, day or night."

I could have taken away all the positives in what he'd just said. Instead, I hung on to his comment about me being a good friend. I supposed he was right. It was what we were and what we'd always be. It was a fact I'd come to accept long ago.

"I'll speak to you soon, okay?" I said.

"Arrivederci, Georgiana. Tu sei sempre nel mio cuore."

He hung up, and I did a quick internet search of the sentiment he'd just spoken before I forgot it. I was surprised to learn its meaning. He'd said: *You are always in my heart.*

And *he* had always been in mine.

26

I checked in with Harvey the next morning and then headed to my mother's house to see Phoebe, who had decided it was best to remain with our mom instead of returning home. If the roles were reversed, my mother's home wouldn't have been my first, second, or tenth choice of places to stay, but I understood why it was Phoebe's. She had always been Mom's favorite.

My mother opened the door with a hand on her hip and a frown of disapproval on her face. It was a look I knew well and one she'd perfected over the years. It wasn't the first time I'd been greeted in such a manner, and I was certain it wouldn't be the last.

I wanted to say: *What is it this time?*

I didn't.

"Is this how it's going to be, Georgiana?" she asked.

"I don't know, Mom," I said. "How is it?"

"You may be back in town, but it still feels like you're gone. You haven't stopped in for days. You haven't called. There are people here who need you. While you're out gallivanting around, *I'm* here with your sister, day in and day out. She's deteriorating, you know. She's a complete wreck. The least you could do is support her in her time of need."

My mother acted like it was an inconvenience to care for Phoebe on her own, but it was all an act. She relished feeling needed in times of crisis.

"I'm not *gallivanting* around. I'm doing my best to find Lark."

My mother threw her hands in the air. "How would we know? This is the first time you've stopped by since the day you got here."

I had just about reached my threshold, the place where the respect I had for her went out the window.

"Are you finished?" I asked.

She cocked her head to one side. "Yes. Now get in here, spend some time with your sister, and stop being a stranger, okay? We're family. We all need to band together right now."

My mother backed away from the door and allowed me inside. She kissed my cheek and said, "You know I love you, right? I dislike having to take a tone with you like I just did. I wouldn't do it if I thought you didn't need to hear it."

Sure, Mom. Whatever you say.

She always knew the perfect thing to say to make me feel like I was thirteen years old again.

I entered the living room and found Phoebe flipping through channels on the television.

Without looking in my direction, she stood and said, "I've been trying to call you all morning."

"I know," I said.

"You haven't checked in. You haven't told me what's going on or what you've found out, and I've had to get all of my updates from Harvey. It isn't okay, Gigi. It's Thursday. I haven't heard from you in three days."

Round two of family shaming had begun.

"I invited you to come stay with me," I said.

She flashed me a look like she'd just called my bluff. I *had* invited her to stay with me, and the offer was genuine, but we both knew I hoped she'd decline. I wanted to help her in any way she needed, but living together, even for a few days in a tiny mobile home, wasn't a good idea. I was the kind of person who needed a lot of alone time in order to function. Without it, I behaved like a caged animal trying to claw my way to my freedom.

"You can't go this long without letting me know what's going on," she said. "Not this time. Not when my daughter is missing."

My mother walked into the room and folded her arms, nodding in agreement.

Phoebe was right.

They both were.

I hadn't checked in.

It wasn't because I didn't want to see her or talk to her or ask how she was doing. It was because I had nothing of significance to tell her. I had nothing to report. She was desperate for answers, and I didn't have any.

I threw my arms around her and hugged her. She remained stiff with her arms at her sides.

"You're right," I said. "I'm sorry. I wanted to see you when I had good news, and I don't have any yet. I didn't consider that you'd want to see me either way. I'll do better from now on, okay?"

She took a step back and nodded. "Why are you here now?"

"I wanted to ask a few questions about your neighbors."

"Which neighbors?" she asked.

"Mitch and Holly Porter."

"What do you want to know about them?"

"I went to see Hattie yesterday. She seems to think the man who ran by her house the other night had the same build as Mitch Porter."

"Are you saying she believes the guy she saw *was* Mitch?"

"She thinks it *wasn't* Mitch. It was just an observation. Could have been anyone, I suppose."

"I don't care what she thinks or what she doesn't. It wasn't him."

"How can you be so sure?"

"I know him. He'd never harm Jack, and he wouldn't take Lark."

"Why don't you like Holly Porter?"

She sat back on the sofa and crossed one leg over the other. "Hey, Mom, I feel like I need to eat something. Could you make me a salad?"

My mother twisted up her face like she was annoyed. She wanted to stay and soak up every salacious detail. But she'd never been any good at refusing Phoebe anything.

My mother nodded and exited the room.

I sat next to Phoebe.

"What is it?" I asked.

"I was wrong," she said.

"About what?"

"Holly. I thought she liked Jack."

"Why?"

"She'd do things sometimes like rest her hand on his arm or run her hand down his back. I was miffed about it for a while. I'm over it now."

"How do you know she *didn't* like him?"

Phoebe lowered her voice. "Because she started doing it to me too."

The conversation had taken an unexpected turn.

"You're saying Holly started touching your arm and stuff?"

"Yeah. She's an expressive person. The more I clued in to it, the more I realized she did it to everyone, and I'd stewed over it for no reason. I'm not saying she's my favorite person. She's a bit odd, but she's harmless."

I wasn't sure why the news was something my mother couldn't hear. Phoebe hadn't said anything remarkable—yet.

"Maybe Holly realized you'd witnessed her hands-on approach and decided it would be best to do it to you too, so you didn't suspect she had feelings for Jack," I said.

Phoebe leaned in closer and lowered her voice. "Holly loves Mitch, but she, umm … she also loves women. She wasn't attracted to Jack. She was attracted to me. Still is, I think."

Of all the things I thought she might say, Holly's feelings for women wasn't one of them.

"How did you find out?" I asked.

"She told me a while back, after you'd gone. She knew I was acting weird toward her, and she thought it was because I realized she'd flirted with me from time to time. I hadn't, though. When someone is interested in me, I tend to be the last one to notice."

"Does her husband know?" I asked.

She nodded. "He's cool with it. She doesn't act on it, I don't think, not since they've been together."

My mother returned with the salad, which could have earned her a gold medal for being made in record time.

She smiled at us as if to say, *"What did I miss?"*

I had another question for Phoebe, one I'd hoped to ask before my mother returned, but I hadn't been fast enough, and it had to be asked.

"Phoebe," I said, "did you know Jack hired a private investigator?"

Her eyes widened.

She didn't know.

"What?" she said. "When?"

"In the weeks before he died."

"Who told you he hired a private investigator?"

"Terry Pearson."

"Oh. Well, if Terry said it, then Jack must have."

"Why on earth would he hire a PI?" my mother asked.

"I don't know," I said. "I'm meeting with the guy later today."

I wanted to probe my sister further over her relationship with Jack to see if she might change her tune now that he'd passed away. But she'd never tell me anything different in front of our mother. It would have to wait.

"Does … uhh … Willy have a tendency to hide things in his cat bed?" I asked.

She rolled her eyes. "All the time. Drives me nuts, I swear. It started with him wandering around at night and bringing back random things he found in the neighbors' yards. He'd leave the trinkets in the doorway of my room. I had no idea where they came from, so I started throwing them away. Then he scratched a hole in his bed and started hiding things there. I've replaced his bed three times in the last six months."

"I found something interesting in his bed last night. I've dropped it off to the coroner for processing."

"What was it?"

"A money clip with the initials TP on it." I took out my cell phone, scrolled through a few photos, and turned the phone toward her. "Any chance you recognize it?"

Phoebe and my mother leaned in.

"I've never seen it before," Phoebe said.

"Me either," my mom said.

"It's possible it fell out of the man's pocket when he was running," I said. "and Willy found it and hid it in his bed."

"A cat sleuth," my mother said. "Who knew? Maybe Willy saw the whole thing. Too bad pets can't talk, eh?"

Phoebe glanced across the room at a framed picture sitting on top of my mother's piano. In the photo, Lark held a blue ribbon from winning first place in a cupcake contest at last year's fair. Phoebe stared at the photo until her eyes blurred, and then she looked away.

My mother swiped the photo off of the piano and opened a drawer to stick it inside.

"No, Mom, don't," Phoebe said. "If you put it away, it's like we've given up on her. It's like she's already dead."

Tears gushed from Phoebe's eyes, and I grabbed her hand. "I will find her, Phoebe. I will bring her home."

My phone buzzed, and I looked down to see a message from Hattie. It said: *I need you to come over please. Today. Not three days from now.*

I replied and said I'd be there soon.

I stayed with Phoebe until she calmed down and then said my goodbyes and headed outside to find my brother's car pulling up in the driveway.

Great.

I wasn't in the mood to deal with which chameleon Tasha was today. Paul got out of the car, and I breathed a sigh of relief. He appeared to be alone.

"Hey, sis," he said.

"What are you up to today?"

"The usual. You?"

He held up a paper sack from In-N-Out. "Just went for a burger run."

I checked the time.

It was just before eleven in the morning.

"It's a bit early for hamburgers, isn't it?" I asked.

"We don't all get our daily protein from eggs." He grinned. "I have an extra burger in the bag if you're interested. Want one?"

"Thanks, I'm fine."

"Are you?"

"Are *you*?" I asked. "How are things with Tasha?"

"They aren't. Wish you wouldn't have told her to talk to me about how she's been feeling."

"Why not? She needed to get it out."

"I was kinda hoping the conversation could wait. There's a lot going on right now. I wanted to deal with it later. Guess it's too late now."

It seemed I didn't compare to Dear Abby after all.

"What happened?" I said.

He set the bag on top of the car, leaned against it, and ran a hand through his hair. "Guess I might as well say it. You'll all find out soon anyway."

"Find out what?"

"We broke up last night."

So far, my only success had been in becoming a wrecking ball.

"Isn't there anything the two of you can do to work it out?" I asked.

He shook his head. "I'm done, Gigi. I don't want to be married to her anymore."

"Why? Is it because she accused you of sleeping with someone else?"

"No … yeah … maybe. Gosh, I don't know. And she's wrong, by the way. I haven't slept with anyone else. I'm not having an affair."

"She said you lied to her about going to a basketball game with one of your friends."

"Yeah, well, my buddy backed out at the last minute, and I decided I'd go alone. If I had told Tasha he wasn't coming, she would have invited herself to come with me. I shouldn't have lied, but we'd been having problems, and I needed some time to myself."

"If Tasha hadn't accused you of having an affair, would it still be over between you two?"

He nodded. "What's happened with us … it's not about any one thing. It's about a lot of things. I stayed quiet when I should have spoken up, put up with things I shouldn't have tolerated. We resided in the same house together, but it's been over between us for a while now. For me, at least."

"It was a shock to hear she slept with Liam."

Paul shrugged. "I don't blame her for what she did, and I don't blame Liam, either. I've been checked out of our marriage for a long time. I wasn't giving her the attention she needed, so she found it with someone else. She felt abandoned by me. I don't think she meant for it to happen. It just did."

Paul had always been the most levelheaded, honest member of our family, and today was no exception.

"I'll support you either way," I said. "I just want you to be happy. How do you feel about your decision?"

"I feel, I dunno, free, I guess. Freer than I've felt in a long time." He grabbed the bag off the top of the car and headed in my direction. "Better get these burgers inside before they get cold. By the way, guess who I ran into this morning?"

"Who?"

"Tiffany Wheeler."

"I'm not surprised she's here. I may have given her card to someone yesterday."

"Yeah, she said you did. She's taking the case, I guess. Who's she representing?"

"Jack's former clients."

It was much easier than saying they were the people responsible for the fire at Jack's office and the death of his assistant.

"Did she say anything else?" I asked.

"She said she hadn't heard from you in a while and was glad to hear you're back in town. You should give her a call."

"Once I've found Lark, I will."

"I'm here for you, you know, if you, uhh … need me for anything."

"I know. You're a good brother, Paul. I'd love to stick around and talk more, but I have somewhere I have to be now. Maybe later?"

He nodded. "Sure, give me a ring when you're free. I'm around."

27

Hattie was in her front yard when I arrived, dressed in a long, thick, hot-pink robe. She had a large cluster of foam curlers rolled into various sections of her hair, which she'd tucked beneath a clear shower cap. She was spraying water over her flower garden, even though it was filled with more weeds than flowers by a ratio of three to one. I wasn't sure why she'd chosen today to resurrect the neglected blossoms, but I suspected she was outside because she was anxious for my arrival.

"It took you long enough to get here," she said.

"It's been less than an hour, Hattie. I came as soon as I could. What's going on?"

"I have something for you."

"What is it?"

"Come inside, and I'll show you."

"I have a lot to do today. Can't we just get straight to the part where you tell me why you asked me to come over here?"

She switched the water off and rolled the hose back onto the reel, like it was delicate and the only thing she needed to do for the rest of the day.

"You could do with some manners, Georgiana," she said. "I'm just trying to help."

And she could do with getting to the point.

"I'm just trying to figure out why I'm here," I said. "You still haven't given me a straight answer."

"It's always rush, rush, rush when it comes to you. Do you ever stop for a minute and breathe or take the time to look around? You might see how much life you're missing if you did."

I stopped when I needed to stop.

Right now, I needed to go.

"Why am I here?" I asked.

She shuffled past me and motioned for me to follow her inside the house. We walked into her craft room, and she riffled through various items all over the top of her desk and muttered, "Hmm. Where has it gone to now? It was just here. Yes, yes, I'm sure it was. I set it on the desk, and then I sent you the text, and now it appears to have disappeared."

I sighed.

It was going to be a long day.

"*What* has disappeared?" I asked.

"Oh, right. I remember what I did with it now. My desk was such a mess, and I wanted to put it in a safe place so I wouldn't lose it, so I stuck it on the refrigerator. I swear, my head is just not screwed on all the way these days."

The refrigerator.

Got it.

I pivoted and walked out of the room.

"Hang on," she called after me. "Wait just a minute. Wait for me."

I kept on going, reached the refrigerator, and noticed it wasn't much more organized than the desk. I guesstimated she had at least fifty magnets of all shapes and sizes covering the door, and half of them were in use.

"What am I looking for, Hattie?" I asked.

She held a hand out in front of her. "Stand aside, and I'll show you."

I slid to the right and bit my tongue a few moments longer.

"All right, now," she said. "I think, yes, yes. It's here. Found it."

She removed a colorful magnet of the city of San Francisco off a piece of folded paper and then presented the paper to me like it was a precious commodity.

"Here it is," she said. "Here's what I wanted to show you."

She was proud. So proud.

"You wanted to show me a piece of scratch paper? Why?"

"Open it up. Go on."

I slid the paper open and lifted it to my face. There, written in bold, black ink were the words: *I'm ready to reveal myself to you, but you need to come home. Come home, Phoebe, and we'll get through this together.*

28

"Where did you get this piece of paper, Hattie?" I asked.

"It was on Phoebe's car," she said. "I was out for my morning walk, and I noticed something beneath her windshield wiper. I went over to take a look and found this note. Couldn't believe what it said. I mean, what is going on with Phoebe and this mystery man of hers? Can you believe it? Can you imagine what ran through my mind when I realized Phoebe has been cavorting with someone else while her—"

"You don't know what you're talking about, and you should have left the note where it was when you found it, called me, and waited for me to get here. It's evidence."

"Well, golly gee. I was just trying to help. You don't have to be rude about it."

"I'm not trying to be. I just …"

I just was getting more frustrated by the second.

"What time did you go out for your walk?" I asked.

"Ten minutes before I sent you the text."

"Did you see anyone around that you didn't recognize, on the street or in a car, or anything?"

"Nope, not a soul." She drummed her fingers on the kitchen counter. "Well, come to think of it, I did see *one* person."

She paused without giving the name, which seemed to be for effect. Part of me wanted to wrap my hands around her neck and shake her senseless.

"Who did you see?" I asked.

"Holly Porter. She backed out of her driveway and was taking her boy to school when I passed."

"Did she say anything to you?"

"Of course. She said hello. She always says hello when she sees me."

"Did she say anything else?"

"She asked if I'd heard from Phoebe and if I knew when she'd be back. She also said she saw you at my place and wondered what was going on with the investigation. She's a right curious sort, that Holly. Always asking questions."

"Did you tell her about the note you found?"

"I, uhh ... well, the thing is ..."

She had.

"Forget it," I said. "I'm not interested in an explanation. I need a plastic bag. Do you have one?"

"I might."

She pulled three of her kitchen drawers open before she located a single plastic bag stuck behind a roll of foil. She handed it to me, and I slipped the note inside.

"I gotta go," I said.

"All righty. If I see another note, I'll give you a call first, okay?"

"You won't see one. I'm taking Phoebe's car."

"Why would you go and do something like that?"

I walked out the front door and didn't look back. "Goodbye, Hattie."

29

Holly Porter was an attractive woman. She was a couple inches taller than I was, about five foot ten, and she had long, wavy, blonde hair and deep blue eyes. At first glance, everything about her seemed fake. Fake eyelashes, fake nails, fake hair color, and what I guessed were fake boobs. She was dressed in a long, yellow dress with white polka dots and looked like a Southern Belle Barbie version of a Stepford Wife.

"You're Phoebe's sister, right?" she asked.

"Right," I said.

"Are you here about the note? Hattie told me about it."

"I'm … no. I'm here to talk about the investigation."

She looked me over. "I love your dress. Where'd you get it?"

Today I was dressed in a black, chiffon, midi V-neck dress with a gray waistband. It may have been a bit dressy for work, but it fit my mood for the day.

"I bought it from a vintage dress shop online," I said.

"Oh, I see. How's Phoebe doing?"

"Fine."

"I'd like to see her. Do you think she's up for visitors?"

"I'm not sure. I'll talk to her, and she can reach out to you if she feels up to seeing anyone."

"I appreciate it. What can I do for *you*, honey?"

She said *honey* like she was my elder, even though I had at least five years on her.

"I wanted to talk to you about the night Jack was murdered," I said.

She frowned. "It's fine. I can talk about it. I just don't like dwelling on things I find unpleasant. Gives me bad dreams at night."

It didn't stop me from questioning her anyway.

"What was Jack like on the night he died?" I asked.

"He seemed to be in a good mood. Of course, he's always seemed pleasant when I've been around."

"You didn't notice anything out of the ordinary?"

She thought about it. "Do you want to come in and sit down? I was just about to make a raspberry mojito."

I shook my head. "I'm working."

"Oh, there's no alcohol in it. I don't drink. It's made with raspberry, mint, syrup, cranberry juice, lime, and club soda. What do you think? Want to try one?"

I did.

"Thanks, but I have a lot to do today," I said.

"Oh, come on. You'll love it. I can whip them up in no time."

She placed a hand on my wrist. I jerked it back.

"Can you just answer the question?" I said.

She frowned. "Your sister told you, didn't she?"

"Told me what?"

"What I told her. Guess no one knows how to keep a secret anymore."

"I knew there had been friction between you two," I said, "so I questioned her about it this morning. She didn't intend to break your confidence. She wanted me to know she'd been wrong about you, and she thought telling me the truth was the best way."

"She misjudged me, like you did just now when I touched your arm. I'm not attracted to every woman I see, you know, just like you're not attracted to every guy *you* see. I may be flirtatious, but I love my husband."

"I understand," I said. "Where is your husband? I need to speak to him too."

"He's not here. Went fishing for the day with his friend Sam."

"When will he be back?"

"They're staying overnight in a tent. He'll be back in the morning. I'll tell him you'd like to speak to him."

"I appreciate it," I said.

"You should know, after you left town, Phoebe and I cleared the air. She confided in me because you weren't here. We became good friends, and I'd never do anything to jeopardize our friendship. The last night I saw Jack, he was fine. A bit preoccupied, but nothing unusual. There. I've answered your question. And I have things to do, so ..."

She started to close the door, and I placed my hand against it.

"I didn't mean to upset you," I said.

"You know something? I looked forward to meeting you. I invited you inside because I thought we might be able to talk about Phoebe and how hard it was on her after you took off. I figured if I explained what she never will, it might help you to know how bad she felt about the argument you two had before you left. She wanted to be there for you and what you were going through, and she felt shut out."

"Guess Phoebe didn't keep my secrets, either."

She shrugged. "Guess not."

I handed her a card with my details on it. "Give this to your husband and thank you."

"For what?"

"Being there for Phoebe when I wasn't."

30

decided it was my turn to stalk my sister's stalker. I penned a short note in response to the one he'd left and suggested the two of us meet at the park that evening at seven beneath a huge oak tree in the park's center. Then I drove Phoebe's car to her workplace, parked it in her assigned spot, and placed the note beneath the wiper. I took a taxi back to Phoebe's and retrieved my Jeep, which I had stowed in the garage to keep it out of sight.

I debated whether or not to call Phoebe and speak to her about the note Hattie had found. I didn't want to tell her about it, but I'd promised to keep her informed, and my word was everything. I'd also been swayed by the fact Hattie and Holly both knew about the note already, and I didn't need one of them telling her about it before I did.

The call with Phoebe didn't go as planned and ended with her asking to tag along for the unveiling of her stalker. I said no. She said it didn't matter whether I wanted her there or not. She wanted to know his identity. She was going.

I had a couple of hours to kill, so I drove back by Phoebe's work to see if the bait I'd set had any takers. I was disappointed to see the note where I'd left it. Maybe he'd be a no-show and tonight wouldn't happen. A few more hours would provide the answer.

I stopped at Andy Sanders' office for our five o'clock appointment. He wasn't there. I waited several minutes and then called his cell phone. It rang a few times and went to voicemail. I'd been stood up, and I didn't like it. I left him a voicemail saying he had a few hours to get back to me before I tracked him down at his home.

I drove by Phoebe's office a third time, and the note was gone, but I found Joseph Coldwell standing next to Phoebe's car with his hand cupped against the driver's-side window.

"See anything of interest in my sister's car?" I asked.

He turned, shocked to see me walking in his direction.

"Detective," he said. "What are *you* doing here?"

"Why are you lurking around Phoebe's car?"

"I was on my way out, and I saw it parked here, and I wondered why. It shouldn't be here. So, why is it?"

I shrugged. "Maybe she stopped by to grab something out of her office or to visit her coworkers. Who knows?"

"I was just in the office. I didn't see her."

He'd balled up one of his hands into a fist.

Was he hiding something?

"What do you have there?" I asked.

He looked around. "Where?"

"In your hand."

He lifted his right hand. "Nothing."

"Your *other* hand."

He opened his left hand and jingled a set of keys in front of me. "Satisfied?"

No. I wasn't.

"Have you called Phoebe about her job?" I asked. "We agreed

you'd welcome her back when all this is over, and she hasn't said she's heard from you."

"She hasn't."

"Why not?"

"You asked for a list of names, and I supplied it."

"I asked for a list *and* for Phoebe's job to be secure when she's ready to return to work."

He sighed. "Yeah, well, we can't always have what we want in life. I've decided to go in another direction."

Another direction?

I don't think so.

"Meaning?" I asked.

"It's a bummer, what happened to your sister, but it's not the network's fault. We have to keep going, no matter what the circumstances may be. We can't wait for her to recover, to get past what she's going through right now."

"Get to the point."

"Fine. I've hired someone else."

"A temp. I know. Malorie Morgan. She can step aside when Phoebe steps back in."

He shook his head. "Malorie's ratings are better than Phoebe's were before she left. We're keeping her on. She'll assume Phoebe's position as of next week."

I'd given him a chance. If he had just taken the high road, what I was about to say wouldn't have needed to be said. But people never seemed to relish the easy way out as much as the challenging one.

Ah, well. His loss.

"The high ratings you claim Malorie's getting," I said. "Are we talking news ratings, or the rating you've been giving her in the bedroom?"

He looked like he was two seconds away from putting me into a headlock, and I hadn't even fired my biggest gun yet.

"What are you ... How dare you say what—"

"How dare I speak the truth, you mean?"

He pointed toward the exit of the garage. "You need to leave. Right now."

"Every other Tuesday and the occasional Friday night," I said.

He stepped back, eyed me, and said, "What?"

"The Airbnb you rent three or four times a month. Well, except for when your wife is out of town, and then you use your own house for liaisons because ... well, it's a lot more convenient and discreet, and it saves money, right?"

His face flushed, going from a bright Strawberry Shortcake to a pasty white.

My message had been received.

"The feeling you're experiencing right now?" I said. "If you don't recognize it, let me help you out. You're in shock."

"I ... How do you know ..."

I reached out and patted him on the shoulder. "Hey, it's okay. I get it. Lots of people step out on their spouses nowadays. I'm sure the two of us could sit down with your wife and clear all of this up in a jiffy. Not today. I have somewhere else to be after we're finished. What's your schedule like tomorrow? I should be able to squeeze the two of you in for a few minutes."

"Whatever you think you know—you can't prove it."

"I can, or I wouldn't use it against you now. Remember the day I sat in your office and waited for you to arrive? I wasn't just sitting. I was sorting through all of the items on your desk. You can learn a lot about a person by looking at their bills and how they spend their money. Do I need to elaborate?"

He bent over Phoebe's car and began wheezing.

Perhaps I'd gone too far.

I thought about why it had been so important to me to secure my sister's job when she hadn't even said whether she planned to go back to it. I'd just assumed she would. I was a fixer. I liked fixing things. When I was weighted down with guilt, I liked fixing even more. It made me feel better about the injustice I'd done.

"You gonna be okay?" I asked.

He reached in his jacket pocket and pulled out an inhaler. He pressed it to his lips and sucked in the medicine. He steadied his breathing, looked at me, and said, "You are a disgraceful, vicious woman. But you keep my wife out of this, and I'll give you what you want."

31

et's go over what's going to happen when we get to the park," I said.

Phoebe tugged at the cardigan she was wearing, wrapping it so tight around the front of her it looked like she might struggle to breathe.

"You don't have to do this," I said. "You don't have to go. I can find out who this guy is on my own."

"I *do* need to do it," she said. "What if he knows where Lark is?"

"Then I'll make sure he tells me."

"I … no. I want to be there with you when he shows up."

We drove for a few minutes in silence, and then I pulled the Jeep to a stop next to a broken lamppost. I killed the ignition and turned toward her.

"I go first," I said. "You stay behind me. Got it?"

She nodded.

"I mean it, Phoebe," I said. "No matter what happens, I need you to let me make the first move. Understand?"

"Yeah, yeah. Can we get this over with now?"

We were six minutes away from our scheduled meeting time with Phoebe's stalker. Not far from the oak tree, Hunter was already in position, something I'd requested hours before—in the event we had a runner, and I needed backup. She'd arrived thirty minutes before I had, so I gave her a quick call to find out if she'd experienced any premature action on her end.

"See anything yet?" I asked.

"A few people here and there," Hunter said. "Nothing suspicious. No one has gone anywhere near the oak tree so far."

"We just arrived and are about to head over."

"Sounds good."

I ended the call.

Phoebe grabbed the door handle.

"Wait a minute," I said.

I reached into the back seat and grabbed a black satchel I'd stowed behind it. I popped it open, pulled out the items I was after, and spruced up my look.

Phoebe's eyes widened. "What are you doing?"

I turned to her and smiled. "I paid good money for this wig. I think it looks similar to your hairstyle. You don't like it?"

She reached out and ran a hand through my fake hair. "It's … ahh … a lot thicker than mine, and this isn't how I wore my hair at work."

I pulled the hair back into a loose bun to mimic her business style and tried again. "How about now? Any better?"

"It won't work."

"It *will* work."

"He'll know it isn't me. I mean, maybe we're similar in height and body type, but …"

"It's dark out, Phoebe. Height and body type are all he needs to see to think it's you. I'll stay in the shadows at first. By the time he figures out I'm not you, it will be too late."

I removed a pair of dress slacks from the bag, pulled them on, and tucked the bottom of my dress into my waistband, transforming the dress into a shirt. My look was almost complete.

"I need your cardigan," I said.

She shook her head. "I ... don't want to take it off."

"Come on. It's just for a few minutes."

She huffed an irritated, "Fine," unwrapped it, and dropped it into my lap. She pulled her arms across her body like she was hugging herself. The cardigan was more than an article of clothing. It offered her a sense of security, like long hair draped over part of a person's face. Without it, she felt naked.

"You going to be all right?" I said.

"Yep, yeah. I'm fine."

"Good. Let's go."

We exited the Jeep and inched toward the oak tree. I didn't want to get too close too soon and risking the stalker seeing both of us and getting spooked.

"All right," I said, "this is far enough. We'll wait it out here behind these bushes.

Phoebe stared at the bushes and then looked at the oak tree. "How are we supposed to see him? We're not close enough."

I pulled a small pair of binoculars out of my bag. "We're as close as we need to be for now. Trust me. Okay?"

Five minutes went by, and then ten, and then twenty.

"I don't think he's coming," she said. "I can't believe it. This was all for nothing."

"Let's give him a few more minutes before we give up."

"I don't see why. If he was going to be here, he would be."

I sighed. She was right. The stalker's last note suggested he was anxious to meet her. He should have been early, not late.

I lifted my phone out of my bag, looked at it, and then slipped it back inside.

"What are you doing?" she asked.

"I swore my phone buzzed a few minutes ago. I guess it didn't. I have no missed calls and no messages."

She slid her hand into her back pocket. "I don't think it was your phone. I think it was mine."

"Why don't you check it?" I asked.

"We're busy. Besides, I'm sure it's just Mom looking for an update because she doesn't know what we're doing."

Phoebe's phone vibrated again. She looked at it this time and then grabbed my arm.

"What is it?" I asked.

"It's *him*. I think it is, at least. He's never texted me before."

"Show me."

She turned the screen toward me. She'd received two missed text messages from an unknown number. The first said: *Are you here yet? Are you still coming?*

It was sent fourteen minutes ago.

The follow-up message that had just come in said: *Guess you changed your mind. I get it. I'll hang out a few minutes longer. Then I'm leaving.*

"Text him back," I said.

"And say what?"

I lifted the binoculars to my eyes and scanned the area.

The perimeter around the tree was empty.

He was waiting, playing it safe.

"Tell him you're here," I said. "Tell him you didn't see him at the oak tree and thought he was a no-show."

While Phoebe worked on the message, I texted Hunter with an update.

Phoebe finished the message, sent it, and said, "What now?"

"We wait for his reply."

A response came within seconds: *I'm ready to meet if you are. I'm so nervous. Are you?*

Phoebe replied with: *Yeah, see you in a minute.*

Twenty feet away from the oak tree, a shadowy figure came into view.

"I see him," I said. "He's heading for the tree."

"What does he look like?"

"Hard to tell yet. From what I can make out so far, he has long hair, and it's pulled back into a ponytail. Looks like he's walking with a bit of a limp."

To me, he looked young, but my definition of young was broad and included anyone between drinking age and their mid-thirties.

"He has a limp?" Phoebe said.

"Looks like it. Mean anything to you?"

When she didn't respond, I faced her and noticed her eyes sparked with recognition.

"You know who he is, don't you?" I said.

"I mean, I might … but it can't be."

She snatched the binoculars out of my hand, gazed through them, and gasped.

"What is it?" I asked.

"You gotta be kidding me," she said. "Sandwich Delivery Guy?"

"Who is *Sandwich Delivery Guy?*" I asked.

The answer to my question would have to wait.

Phoebe had tossed the binoculars onto the grass and took off running.

32

I charged toward Phoebe, even knowing I wouldn't catch *her* before *she* caught *him*. She'd been on the track team in high school and in college and ran in the Asics marathon in Los Angeles each year. Glancing over my shoulder, I noticed we weren't alone. Hunter was sprinting in our direction too.

Phoebe reached the guy and catapulted toward him, tackling him to the ground. Once he was pinned down, she straddled him and began slapping his face while shouting a string of words I couldn't understand. I threw my arms around her shoulders and yanked back, a gesture that infuriated her. Free from Phoebe's wrath, the young man crossed his arms over his face and shielded himself from the possibility of a second round of attacks.

Phoebe jerked back and forth, trying to free herself from my grip. When it wasn't a success, she screamed, "Let me go! This is between him and me. Back off, Gigi!"

"No," I said. "You can't take your anger out on him. Not like this."

"Why can't I? You've done it plenty of times. You do whatever you want whenever you want. Why is it different when it's me?"

"Before we do anything, we need to question him."

"He's guilty. Nothing else matters."

Hunter leaned against a nearby tree, caught her breath, and blinked at me, confused. It took me a minute to realize why and then it clicked.

"It's a disguise, Hunter," I said, "a wig."

"I mean, yeah," she said. "I can, ahh … see that."

I tipped my head toward the Sandwich Delivery Guy. "Hunter, I need you to restrain him until I figure out who he is and what's going on here."

Hunter nodded.

"Let go of me," Phoebe said.

"Not yet," I said.

She jerked her head in the guy's direction and yelled, "Where is she? Where's my daughter? Tell me what you did with her you creep!"

He waved his hands in front of him. "Whoa, wait a minute. I don't know anything about your daughter. I would never hurt her or you, I swear. You believe me, Phoebe, don't you? Tell me you believe me."

I glared at the kid. "Shut up for a minute, mmm…kay?"

It looked like he was about to say something else. I narrowed my eyes, and he kept his trap shut.

"Who is he, Phoebe?" I asked.

"He's the sandwich delivery guy from work."

"What's his name?"

"I don't know. Ask him what it is. I can't remember."

He frowned at Phoebe. Whatever idyllic notions he'd had of the two of them running off together had just been shattered.

"Phoebe?" he asked.

Phoebe shrugged. "What? I have no flipping idea what your name is. And if you think I ever liked you, you're an idiot."

My plan of conducting an interrogation without being interrupted wasn't working. I looked at Hunter and said, "Let's try something different. You take my sister while I take a walk with the kid here."

"I'm not a kid," the kid said.

"Take her *where*?" Hunter asked.

"To your car," I said. "Stay with her until I'm finished here."

"I'm not going anywhere," Phoebe said.

I leaned forward and whispered, "Don't test me, Phoebe. You may be my sister, but right now, you're keeping me from what I'm trying to do here."

She took in a deep breath, stood still for a moment, and then her face softened.

I didn't trust it.

"I want to stay," she said. "Please. I have a right to hear what he says. After all I've been through, don't deny me this, okay?"

"I can't do my job with you here. You keep getting in the way."

She nodded. "I understand. I won't cause any more trouble. Just give me one more chance."

I wanted Hunter to take her home so I could take him to the station, and we could talk without further distractions. Phoebe hadn't done what I'd asked. If she had, we wouldn't have been dealing with the mayhem we were now.

Decisions.

Decisions.

I handed Phoebe off to Hunter. "Don't attack him again, Phoebe. Stand there and keep quiet. Understand?"

She nodded.

I approached the kid. "Who are you? Why have you been stalking my sister?"

"Stalking her?" he said. "What makes you think … I'm not stalking her. I love her."

"You *love* her?"

"Yeah. I mean, I know she's married … well, she *was* married, I guess, but—"

"How old are you?"

"I'll be twenty-eight in three months. Why? Love is love. What does age have to do with it?"

Twenty-seven.

Nine years younger than my sister.

Apparently "love is love" was the way he rationalized stalking a married woman.

"You've been leaving her notes, right?" I asked.

"Yeah."

"And flowers and gifts, and yet you didn't reveal you were the one doing it. If you weren't stalking her, what were you doing?"

"I don't … I didn't mean to …"

I'd pressed his *overwhelmed* button.

"Let's back up and start simple," I said. "What's your name?"

"Zachary Baldwin."

"How do you know Phoebe?"

"I got a job at the television station several months back as an intern for the summer. I'd hoped they would hire me once it was over, but they didn't. They just said they had no positions available, and that was it."

"How did being an intern turn into you stalking Phoebe?"

He brushed some dirt off his arm and said, "Can I sit up?"

I reached out my hand and pulled him to a sitting position.

"Continue," I said.

"On the last day of my internship, I was sitting in the lunchroom. I was bummed out because I liked working there. I didn't want it to be over. It was a mistake for me to assume they'd hire me, but I figured they would. I was so confident about it I'd quit my waiter job."

A stupid move.

"I'm still not sure where Phoebe ties in," I said.

"She walked into the lunchroom to get the food she'd ordered. She saw me sitting alone, looking like the loser I was, and she asked if she could sit by me. We got to talking. I told her what happened, and she placed her hand on mine and said she might be able to help me."

"And did she help you?"

He nodded. "There was nothing she could do about the internship until a position opened up, but one of her friends had just opened a sandwich shop and started delivering to businesses. He was looking to hire a couple of people to help with the deliveries, and the pay was great. She suggested I work for him until a position opened up at the network. Phoebe gave the sandwich-shop guy a call, and he hired me."

It was all starting to make sense.

"I think I understand what happened," I said.

"You do?" he said.

"When Phoebe touched your hand, you assumed she felt something for you."

"She wouldn't have gotten me the job if she didn't want to keep me around. We deliver to her office every day."

Since when was a woman not allowed to touch a member of the opposite sex without them getting the wrong impression?

Since forever.

In her naivety, she'd sent the wrong signal without even knowing it.

"She touched your hand because she felt bad for you," I said. "It's called sympathy, and it's a hell of a lot different than love."

He shook his head. "You're wrong. She cares for me. I know she does."

"I'm not wrong. You need to face facts."

He looked at Phoebe. "Tell her."

"Tell her *what*?" Phoebe said. "There's nothing to tell."

"Tell her about the times I dropped off lunch and you stopped what you were doing to have a conversation with me. Or the time you gave me a piece of cake when one of the guys in the office had a birthday, or the time your assistant called me a cab when the tire on my bike went flat."

A stunned Phoebe stared at him, her jaw dropping open. "You're delusional. I wasn't the one who liked you, you moron. Janet did."

"Janet?" he said. "Your … *assistant?*"

"Think about it," Phoebe said. "I offered you a piece of cake because she was sitting in my office at the time, getting ready to have a piece. If you recall, I handed you a piece and walked out. And I never asked her to call you a cab. She did it because in her own introverted way, she was trying to let you know she liked you."

He bowed his head and said, "No. I can't believe it. It's not true."

Phoebe blinked at me, and I nodded at Hunter, who released the loose grip she had on my sister's arm.

Phoebe knelt next to Zachary and said, "You don't have my daughter, do you? And you didn't kill my husband."

He looked up at her and said, "No, and I'm sorry. I'm sorry for everything."

Phoebe stretched her arms out, bent down, and buried her face in the grass, sobbing. "It's over. We're never going to find her. We're never going to find my baby girl."

It broke me to see her so disheartened.

Once again, I'd come up short.

I asked Hunter to escort Zachary back to the station for further questioning. I wanted to be sure there wasn't something he was hiding or hadn't said. Once they were out of sight, I scooped my sister off the ground. She was like a ragdoll in my arms, lifeless, like she didn't have the will to walk.

"Don't give up on me, Phoebe," I said. "Not yet. I know how you're feeling right now, but I'm going to find her. I—"

"Just stop. Stop it, okay?" she whispered. "Take me back to Mom's. I want to be alone."

The words "alone" and "Mom" were like oil and water—they didn't mix. But I complied with her request. On the way there, she didn't utter a single word, and we spent the entire drive in awkward silence.

When the Jeep rolled to a stop in front of our mom's place, she got out and headed for the door without looking back.

"I'll call you tomorrow," I said. "Let me know if you need anything. Okay?"

She pretended not to hear me. I watched her until she made it into the house, and then my cell phone rang. It was Harvey.

"I just received a call from a frantic woman who said she's found her husband in his study with a bullet in his chest. I'm headed there now."

"Is he dead?"

"Think so."

"What's his name?"

"That's why I'm calling. I believe he's someone you wanted to question. The fellow's name is Andy Sanders. Isn't he the PI Jack hired?"

He was.

It was going to be a long night.

33

Andy Sanders was slumped over his desk with his head resting on a pile of papers when I found him. His wife was sitting on a chair beside him, patting his arm with one hand and sniffling into a tissue with the other. Harvey hovered over her doing his best to keep her calm while Silas explained in the most diplomatic way possible that he needed her to give him a few minutes with her husband so he could examine his body.

So far, the wife hadn't budged, and she appeared to be mumbling to herself.

"I went out for ice cream," she said. "I wasn't going to since we've both been trying to stick to a new diet we're doing together, but he had a craving for butter pecan, and since tomorrow is our cheat day, I thought it wouldn't be a big deal if we started a tad early."

"What time did you leave the house?" I asked.

She looked up at me, startled, like she hadn't noticed me enter the room.

"Who are you?" she asked.

"My name is Detective Germaine."

"Oh. I see. How many more of you will be coming?"

"It's just us for now," I said.

She was on edge.

The present moment didn't seem like the right time to tell her we weren't the only guests she would receive tonight.

"I guess it was around eight thirty or so," she said.

"And what time did you get back?"

"I don't know."

"How long would you guess you were out of the house?"

"Hard to say."

"Did you speak to your husband before you left?" I asked.

"I came into the office, yes."

"What was he doing?"

"I don't know. I didn't ask."

Questioning her wasn't going to be easy.

"I was supposed to meet with your husband today," I said. "When I arrived at his office, he wasn't there."

"What time was your meeting?"

"Five o'clock."

"He would have been there then. Maybe you didn't see him."

"The office door was locked."

"How strange. What was the purpose of your meeting?"

"Have you heard about the murder of Jack Donovan?" I asked.

"The doctor? Sure. I suppose everyone in the state knows about it by now, don't they? It's all people around here are talking about. What does the doctor's death have to do with you meeting my husband?"

"Jack Donovan hired him before he died."

"Why?"

"I'm not sure yet. That's why I wanted to meet with him."

Silas raised a brow to suggest I move our conversation elsewhere.

"I'd appreciate a cup of tea if you have it, Mrs. Sanders," I said. "I'd be happy to make you one too."

She gazed at her husband, now clutching his hand. "I'm not ready to leave him. Not yet."

"Ma'am," Harvey said.

"Polly," she said. "My name is Polly."

"Polly, I know how hard this is, but if Silas here doesn't look your husband over right away, we'll lose valuable information."

"Can't you just … I don't know … go around me?" she asked. "I can sit still."

"We can't," Harvey said. "Now please, let us do our job."

She sighed. "Will it take long? I don't want to be away from my Andy for more than a few minutes."

Polly didn't seem to grasp that her husband wouldn't be staying with her tonight or any other night. Once Silas finished his assessment at the house, Andy would be transported to the morgue for an autopsy.

"Come on, Polly. Let's step out for some tea," I said, "and you can check on your husband after they've finished in here."

She focused on her husband for some time and said, "You'll forgive me, won't you? I won't be long."

Harvey, Silas, and I exchanged glances, but kept quiet.

I'd seen various kinds of mourners in my time, and the more Andy's wife spoke, the more concerned I became about her falling into a category of people who went a bit mad after their loved one died. These types of people were extremists, and often they were so brokenhearted they ended up in a psych ward of some kind. I hoped the judgment I'd just passed on her turned out to be inaccurate. I hoped she was just in shock.

Polly released her husband's hand, nodded at me, and stood. "Let's get to it then."

I followed her out of the study and into the kitchen. She told me where I could find the tea in the pantry. I made us both a cup and joined her on the sofa.

She crossed one leg over the other and said, "I'm not sure I'm up to answering any questions right now. It's all a bit fuzzy, you see."

"Anything you can tell me would be helpful."

"Andy and I have been married for forty-nine years. We celebrate our fiftieth next month, and then he promised to retire after that. We thought we'd take a cruise, the kind you live on for several months. There are so many places I haven't been, so many places I still want to go. What about you? Do you travel?"

"Whenever I can," I said. "I've thought about going to Africa this year."

Polly pressed a hand to her chest. "Africa? Seems a bit scary with all those wild animals running around. I'm not as adventurous, I'm afraid. I've never been much of a risktaker. The cruise I have my eye on goes to Highclere Castle in England."

"What's at Highclere Castle?"

"Downton Abbey, of course. If you've never seen the show, you should. Pity it's no longer on the air."

I had seen the show. Every episode.

"What kind of investigating does your husband do?" I asked.

She took a sip of tea, scrunched up her face, and held the cup out to me. "It needs more honey, dear. Do you mind?"

I took the cup into the kitchen, stirred in a heaping teaspoon of honey, and returned it to her. She sampled it a second time and said, "Hmm … might be a bit *too much* honey now. Ahh, well. Thank you for trying."

"Did your husband discuss his cases with you?" I asked.

"He does not. Well, not many of them, anyway. There was an actress who went missing some decades ago. He was thrilled to get the job and couldn't keep the details of it from me. I won't say whom she was, but she'd been in all kinds of movies. Her disappearance made headlines everywhere. It was a big deal."

"Was the woman ever found?"

"She was, and it turned out she'd had enough of the limelight and just wanted to take a break. Trouble was, she didn't tell anyone. She just left."

"Sounds like he was good at his job."

"You asked before what kind of investigating Andy does. Most of the time he finds people."

"What kinds of people?"

"Anyone who needs to be found. He has a ninety-three percent success rate. People call him from all over the country."

She'd been speaking about her husband like he was still alive, and I wondered how long it would continue.

"How many cases was your husband working on in the last month?"

She shrugged. "I don't know. Like I said, we don't talk much about the details of his work."

"What about his client files? Does he keep them at the office?"

She nodded. "In the bottom drawer of his desk. You'll need a key. I'll get it for you."

Polly scampered down the hall. When she returned, she was dressed in a different nightgown than the one she'd worn a few minutes before. She grabbed her cup of tea, swallowed a mouthful, and then spat the liquid back into the cup.

"My word," she said. "This is awful. Who puts this much honey in a cup of tea?"

I seemed to be in *The Twilight Zone*.

"Polly, is everything all right?" I asked. "Did you find your husband's keys?"

She blinked at me and said, "His keys?"

"Yes. You just went to get them for me."

She reeled back, glaring at me like I was an intruder. "Who are you? What are you doing in my house? How did you get in here?"

The front door opened, and a man around my age rushed to Polly's side. In his hand was a small tub of butter-pecan ice cream.

Nothing made sense.

The man was bald, taller than most, and had the girth of a football player.

"Mom?" he said. "What happened?"

"I … I don't know. What are you doing here?"

"You called me."

"I did? Oh. I must have forgot."

He turned toward me. "What is going on here?"

I thumbed toward the back of the room. "Can I talk to you for a minute?"

He nodded, helped his mother sit down, and then covered her with a purple afghan that had been folded over the couch. We walked about fifteen feet away, far enough to whisper without her hearing the conversation, but close enough for him to watch over her.

"I'm Detective Germaine," I said.

"I'm Robbie," he said.

"Is there something wrong with your mother?"

"Ahh, yeah. She has dementia."

"How long has she had it?"

"She's Stage 5. That's what the doctor says, anyway. Some days she still seems fine. Other days she struggles to remember things that happened five minutes ago. I've been talking to my dad about moving her to a care facility, but he's not ready to let her go yet."

"What does your father do about your mother when he's at work all day?"

"He works part-time now, and next month he's retiring. When he's not here, a home-health nurse I hired looks after her."

"What's her name?"

"*His* name is Lance Woods."

I tipped my head toward the butter pecan. "What's with the ice cream?"

"It's her favorite. Why are you here?"

Down the hall, Silas called my name.

"Can you excuse me for a minute?" I asked.

"I'd like to know what's going on first."

"Give me one minute, and I'll explain everything, all right?"

Harvey entered the room.

"This is Robbie Sanders, Andy's son," I said. "He just arrived."

"Why don't I ... ahh ... talk to him while you talk to Silas?" Harvey said.

I nodded.

Lance raised his voice and said, "Why won't anyone tell me what the hell is going on?"

"No need to use foul language, son," Polly said.

Robbie apologized, and I left Harvey to deal with him.

I entered the study, looked at Silas, and said, "What is it?"

"The timing's off," he said.

"What do you mean?"

"Polly said she was gone for a short time tonight between eight thirty and nine, which meant the murder would have taken place in a thirty-minute window."

"And?"

"It's nine forty-five now, which suggests he'd still be in algor mortis, but he isn't. He's in rigor. Some of the muscles in his body have already stiffened."

He waved me over.

"Take a look at this," he said.

He pointed at Andy's eyelids and then at the neck and jaw area. Silas was right. Andy was in the early stages of rigor mortis.

"You know what this means, right?" Silas asked.

"Yeah," I said. "It means Polly didn't leave to get ice cream when she said she did."

34

ndy was removed from the house to be autopsied, Silas left, and Harvey was overseeing the forensics team on evidence-gathering. I was in the kitchen with Robbie, who had just returned from taking his mother to bed after the sedative he'd given her kicked in. Robbie leaned against the kitchen wall, crossed his arms in front of him, and huffed a heavy sigh.

"How are you doing?" I asked. "You're dealing with a lot right now."

"I'm not sure," he said. "I'm numb, I guess. I don't understand it, any of it. My dad was a nice, decent man. Why would anyone want to kill him?"

"I believe it has something to do with a client who hired him," I said.

"What client? Who is it?"

"I'll explain my theory in a minute. First, I hoped to ask you some questions."

He nodded. "Go on."

"How did you end up coming over here tonight? And why did you bring ice cream?"

"My mom called me about an hour ago. She said she'd been

talking to my dad in his study, and she was upset because he was asleep and wasn't talking back. It made no sense, so I decided to come over and see what was going on."

I wondered if the dementia she suffered from made her think Andy's head resting on the desk was him sleeping.

"What about the ice cream?"

"I bought the ice cream because I always bring it when I visit. It's my mother's favorite, and something we've done together for years."

"She told us she went out to get ice cream earlier."

He shook his head. "There's no way. She doesn't drive anymore. She must have been confused."

"If your mother didn't leave the house tonight, she may have been here when your father was murdered. She may have witnessed it."

"Even if she was, and even if she *did* see someone in the house, I doubt she'll remember. The way her brain works now, when she retells an event, it's like fragments of a story. Some of it's true, and the rest she fills in with whatever happens to be in her imagination at the time. The hardest part is that she believes whatever version of the story she creates, and there's no telling her otherwise. Today she'll tell you one version. Tomorrow she'll tell you another."

"If she was here, I don't understand why the killer would shoot your father and spare your mother."

"Maybe he didn't know she was here. She could have been sleeping."

"Wouldn't a gunshot wake her up?"

"Some of the drugs she takes knock her out. She always naps after lunch, and her room is on the opposite end of the house, a good distance from Dad's study."

"I was supposed to meet your dad at five o'clock today at his office. He didn't show up."

"Did he call you or send a text to let you know why he wasn't there?"

I shook my head.

"He'd never miss a meeting with a client and not get in touch to explain why," he said. "He wouldn't blow you off without a good reason."

"What's your mother's daily routine on the days your father works?"

"Dad spends the first part of the day with Mom, and then Lance arrives after lunch, which is around one o'clock. Once Lance gets here, Dad goes into the office for four hours and then returns home about six to have dinner with Mom before she heads to bed."

"So, Lance would have been here today."

"Yeah, he would have."

"Do you have his number?" I asked.

"I can text it to you."

Robbie sent over Lance's details, and I filled him in on Jack and Lark and why I felt there was a connection to Jack's death and his father's.

"Were you and your dad close?" I asked.

"I'd like to think we were."

"Did he talk to you about the cases he worked on?"

"He wouldn't violate his clients' privacy, even to family, so no. He also didn't discuss the details of the information he found out unless he was face-to-face with the person who hired him."

"Why not?" I asked.

"He could be a bit paranoid at times. With a text message or an email, there was always a chance someone else might see it. With phone calls, someone could eavesdrop. He preferred meeting in person, at the office."

"Your mother said your father keeps his client files locked in the bottom drawer at his office."

"He does."

"She also said I need a key to access it. Any idea where he keeps it?"

"Yep, on his key ring. When he's home, he keeps it in a bowl on the desk in his study. I'd get it for you, but I'm not ready to go in there yet."

"It's okay," I said. "I can get the key."

"The smallest one on the key ring opens the desk drawer, and the other one with a gray band around it unlocks the office."

I nodded, he looked up, and we locked eyes. He was suffering an immense amount of pain—pain he was trying to push down so it didn't bubble to the surface. I'd been there, felt what he was feeling. Standing here now, it was hard to witness.

"I … uhh … I need to call my wife," he said.

"Sure," I said. "I understand."

I walked down the hall and entered the study. There was a metal bowl resting on top of the desk just like Robbie said there would be. The bowl was empty.

"Hey, Harvey," I said.

He eyed me and said, "Yeah?"

"Who bagged the keys that were sitting in this bowl? I don't want them entered into evidence yet. I need them."

"Far as I know, there were no keys in the bowl. It's been empty since I got here."

"What about Polly?" I asked.

"What about her?"

"Did she come back in here after I took her into the living room?"

He shook his head. "No, why?"

"When we were talking earlier, she told me she would get Andy's office keys for me. If she didn't come in here, it means she doesn't have them."

It wasn't hard to guesstimate who did, though.

"The keys aren't all that's missing, then," Harvey said. "When I arrived here, Polly asked me what I did with Andy's laptop. She said he always kept it on the desk. It's not here either."

"What about a cell phone?"

"Nope."

Missing keys.

Missing phone.

Missing laptop.

And missing time I should have spent somewhere else.

"Georgiana," Harvey said, "are you listening?"

I wanted to say I had been, but I hadn't.

He'd continued to talk while I zoned out, a fault I'd had ever since I was a child. Whenever I needed to figure something out, I tuned everyone out. There could be twenty people in a room, and it didn't matter. My thoughts were so loud, they washed them all out.

At the moment, my thoughts were saying I needed to leave.

I needed to get to Andy's office.

Even though I already knew I was too late.

35

ndy's office door was open when I arrived, which meant I was indeed too late. The killer had already been there, taken what he wanted out of Andy's desk, and hit the road. My theory was proved when I found the bottom drawer of Andy's desk open and half of his client files scattered all over the floor. It appeared the killer picked the files out of the drawer and tossed them to the ground until he found the folder he needed.

I gathered the files, stacked them on the desk, and surveyed the rest of the office. The building in which Andy leased his space was made up of six individual offices, each with their own private door on the front. His office was small, no bigger than a standard-size bedroom. Aside from the desk, there were a few bookshelves filled with various books and an end table with a printer on top of it. Based on the sparseness of the room, I doubted I'd find any meaningful clues.

I turned my attention to a datebook resting on the side of the table. Several pages had been torn out of it. I thumbed through it and noticed the entire previous month was missing. It seemed a foolish thing to do. If that month's appointments related to Jack, why not take the whole book instead of leaving me an exact timeline on which I should focus my attention?

"What an idiot," I said out loud, "But hey, thanks for the clue, dude. It's not a lot, but it's better than nothing."

I set the book on top of the files I'd gathered and scanned the office one last time, looking for anything else that seemed relevant before I called Harvey and let him know when the forensics team finished, they weren't done for tonight. They needed to dust Andy's office for prints.

On the second shelf of one of the bookcases, I spied a book turned on its side. I walked over to get a closer look, disappointed when it turned out to be a twenty-two-year-old handbook for private investigators. I was about to put it back when the office lights went out. I supposed the power could have gone out, but through the mini blinds on the opposite wall, the sign advertising the closed fast-food joint across the street was still aglow.

I palmed my gun and backed against the wall next to the bookcase. Then I waited.

I saw nothing.

I heard nothing.

And yet, someone was there.

Someone had killed the light.

A minute passed.

Then two.

And then loud, heavy, breathing emanated from the opposite side of the room.

"I assume you're armed," I said.

A gunshot ripped through the air. It missed me, but not by much. It was close, too close for my liking.

I stepped out and fired in the direction the breathing had come from.

"Looks like we both brought a little something extra to the party," I said. "Where's Lark?"

"Who are you?" a man asked. "Why are you following me?"

"*Where* is Lark?"

"Why are you here?"

His voice was low and muffled, almost like he was trying to disguise it.

"My name's Detective Germaine. What's yours?"

He grunted a laugh. "Snow White."

Ooh, we had ourselves a live one.

"Guess that makes me the Evil Queen," I said. "Find what you were looking for in Andy's office, Snow?"

"Yup. Sure did."

"It doesn't matter, you know. Evidence. No evidence. You're here now, which was your biggest mistake."

"If you want me so bad, come and get me."

What a great suggestion.

I was happy to oblige.

I aimed the gun toward the sound of his voice and squeezed the trigger, hoping to hit him just enough to wound him.

"You shoot like a girl," he said. "Lousy."

"It was a warning shot. If I wanted to kill you, you'd be dead."

Given the office was dark except for the faint glow emanating from the fast-food sign, it was a bold declaration. Too bold, I imagined.

"That's what you're planning to do, kill me?" he asked.

I'd stayed up every night this week thinking about it, so ... yes.

"If you know what's good for you, you won't mess with me."

Of all the lame, tired, cliché phrases I'd heard in my life, the one he'd just uttered made it into my top five, pushing "ignorance is bliss" into the sixth spot. Ignorance *wasn't* bliss. Knowledge was. And okay, yeah, maybe I didn't know what was good for me. I lived for situations like these. Maybe because I didn't value my life the way I once had. Or because fear didn't own me the way it owned other people. Neither did death.

"What happens if I *don't* know what's good for me?" I asked. "What then?"

"You're about to find out."

"Is Lark alive?"

"Maybe."

"Is she still alive?" I asked. "Tell me!"

"What if she isn't?"

Breathe, Georgiana.

Don't put a bullet through his skull.

Not yet.

Keep him talking.

"You could have killed her, and yet you took her instead," I said. "Why? Was kidnapping her your plan all along?"

"She saw me kill her father."

It was possible he had just spilled a significant detail without realizing it. I now believed he'd gone to the house with the intention of killing Jack and *not* taking Lark. At some point, he saw her see him. He could have killed her on the spot. He didn't. It gave me hope she was still alive. But if he was here, where the hell was she?

"*To TP with love.* What does the TP stand for, I wonder? Are they your initials? We found the money clip you dropped. I suppose you realized you'd lost it by now."

"You assume it's mine. What if it isn't?"

"Why did you kill Jack?"

"Because sometimes there's no other way."

"What did he do to deserve death?" I asked.

"He was curious, just like you, and this is what happens to curious people."

A second gunshot rang out. It went through the bookcase and nicked my arm. I bit my lip, stifling a scream. I heard a shuffling sound and assumed he'd abandoned his post and was coming for me. I readied my gun and vacated mine.

Instead of attacking me, he bolted in the opposite direction. I aimed at the sound and pulled the trigger. He howled in pain, and I smiled. Target acquired, although I wasn't sure where he'd been hit.

I leapt forward, running a hand along the wall for the place I thought I'd find the light switch. I was wrong.

He darted out the office door. I chased after him. Once we were outside, it appeared he had been wounded somewhere in his upper body. It wasn't enough to slow him down. He broke into a sprint, heading into a grove of trees.

"Stop!" I said. "Or I'll shoot you again."

He didn't heed my warning.

He ducked inside a truck, threw it into reverse, and floored it, attempting to run me down. I leapt out of the way, my hands scraping the pavement as I tumbled to the ground. On impact, my gun bounced out of my hand, landing a couple of feet away from me. I lunged for it, and he shifted gears, and barreled toward me again. This time when I fired, the bullet burst through the windshield on the driver's side. It was too dark to tell whether it hit him or not, but it was enough to make him rethink his plan of turning me into roadkill. He swerved away from me, his tires squealing as his truck bounced onto the road and sped in the opposite direction.

I raced toward the Jeep, dismayed to find my front tires had been slashed. I slammed my fists onto the hood, again and again and again. I screamed every obscene word that came to mind while reprimanding myself at the same time. I'd had the chance to capture him, and I'd blown it—big time.

Out of options, I called the police station. I hadn't gotten close enough to make out the license plate, but I offered what I believed were the color, make, and model of the truck. Ego broken and my body bruised, I made another call to Harvey, and then I leaned against the Jeep and waited. All I could do now was hope my comrades would find him and succeed where I had failed.

36

It was a blustery, rainy day, the kind of day when the sky ripped open and poured down the feelings I'd kept bottled up inside. The police had searched all night for the man who'd attacked me, scanning the streets of Cambria and its neighboring towns until dawn, but somehow he'd managed to elude us all.

After a restless night and less than two hours of sleep, I woke up feeling drab. A drab inside called for a drab outside, so I dressed in a pair of black, high-waisted, pinstripe suspender pants, a black sleeveless shirt, and black oxford heels.

I'd beaten myself up most of the night for allowing the killer to escape. It was time to work.

First on the agenda was a phone call to Lance Woods, Polly's nurse. He said he hadn't been to Polly's house the day her husband died. He'd felt ill and had called Andy to say he shouldn't come to work. Andy agreed and said he planned to cancel his afternoon appointments. Andy's phone records confirmed he'd received a call from Lance just after one in the afternoon, which lasted two minutes. And since Andy hadn't canceled our meeting, Silas was able to get a much more accurate time of death.

While Luka scarfed up his dog food, I grabbed a manila envelope. It contained the crime scene photos that had been taken the night of Jack's murder. I'd gone over them before and decided I'd do it once again before I headed out. I flipped through them, studying all aspects of each picture.

Jack had been shot through a thin, dark jacket he'd been wearing. In the photos, the jacket was still wet from him falling into the pool, and it was also stained with blood. Close to the bullet's entry point, I noticed something I hadn't before—what appeared to be a small, metal, circular pin. Jack never even wore cufflinks, so the pin was out of place.

I pulled open my side drawer and looked for the pair of bifocals I'd started wearing at night when I read. They weren't there. I slid over to the other side of the bed and reached for the other drawer when a rustling sound outside caused Luka's ears to perk up. He walked to the door and sat in front of it, ready to defend me from the disturbance on the other side.

I was about to go for my gun, when my sister called my name.

I hopped off the bed and opened the door.

She offered me a sandwich inside of a plastic baggie and said, "Here. Mom made it for you."

I dangled the bag in front of me, inspecting its contents. "What is it?"

"A sandwich."

"I know it's a sandwich, Phoebe. What kind?"

"Egg salad. What else?"

It was the first time she'd been sarcastic since I'd returned, and for a moment, I saw a glimpse of my sister again. I'd already eaten an hour before, so I popped the sandwich into the refrigerator for later.

"Tell Mom I said thanks."

She nodded and scanned the interior of my place. "I never thought I'd say this, but for the first time, *you're* the messy one in the family, not me."

"I've been busy, too busy to worry about the clothes I need to put away."

"And dishes, and shoes, and—"

"Point taken," I said. "Want to sit down?"

She searched for an empty space on the sofa. There wasn't one. I grabbed an armful of clothes and tossed them onto the bed.

"There," I said. "You want a drink?"

"Sure. Do you have any white wine?"

"It's nine o'clock in the morning."

"So what? You offered."

"I don't have any white wine."

"Pinot noir, then."

I shook my head. "I have a bottle Tasha gave to me. It's shiraz, though."

She turned up her nose.

"Okay, no shiraz," I said. "What about orange juice?"

She ran a hand through her hair and said, "You've changed."

I sat beside her. "I still drink wine. I just haven't for a while."

"I heard you had a tough night."

I figured it was the reason she was here.

I nodded. "Yeah. I'm sorry."

"For what?"

"I had him, Phoebe. We were in the same room together, and I let him get away."

"You didn't *let him* get away. He ran away, and you shot him."

"Not where I should have. I kept thinking—I could kill this guy, right here, right now. But if I do, how will I ever find Lark? So, I didn't, and now I wish I had."

Phoebe fidgeted with a lock of her hair, winding it around her finger, letting it go, and then winding it back up again. "What's he like, the guy who took her?"

"It was dark. I didn't get a good look at him."

"You talked to him, though, didn't you?"

"For a few minutes. I got the feeling he was trying to disguise his voice, his real voice."

"Why? Do you think you might know him?"

"No," I said. "I think he was trying to sound tough so I wouldn't know he was nervous."

"What did he say to you?"

"He wouldn't tell me anything about Lark or why he killed Jack. He just said Jack had been curious and alluded to the fact that Jack's curiosity got him killed."

"Huh. Jack never seemed curious to me."

"He hired a private investigator," I said. "He was curious about something."

"I've been thinking a lot about why he didn't tell me."

"Perhaps it was for the same reason you didn't reveal you had a stalker."

"I wish I could go back before this all happened and be straight with him. I should have told him from the start."

"Think about Jack's behavior over the last few weeks," I said. "Are you sure you didn't notice anything out of the ordinary?"

She shrugged. "I hate to admit it, but between the changes at work and the stalker, I'd been preoccupied. He could have dyed his hair a different color, and I may not have noticed. I know what you're thinking ... in the end, I was a horrible wife. And you're right."

"You were a good wife, Phoebe. We all check out sometimes. We're human. It's what humans do. I know you loved him."

"What will you do now? How will you find him?"

I wasn't sure.

I'd been asking myself the same question all morning.

"I'm going to stop by your house today," I said.

"Why? They've collected everything they thought was evidence already."

"Sometimes the smallest thing appears to be nothing and turns out to be the key to everything. Speaking of small things, I want to show you something."

I walked to the bedroom, grabbed the photo I'd been looking at before she arrived, and pressed it to my chest so she couldn't see it.

"Before I show you this, I want to make sure you don't mind looking at it," I said. "I know it will be hard."

"Why? What is it?"

"It's a photo of Jack."

"Oh, from the night he died?"

I nodded. "I can cover most of it up and just show you the part I'm wondering about."

"Can you just tell me? I don't ... I mean, I want to help, but I don't want to see it."

"All right. It looks like a small pin he'd placed on his jacket."

"What do you mean—a pin?"

"Like the kind you get when you're a member of a club or an organization. Would he have received something like that as a doctor?"

"I don't think so, and if he had, he'd never wear it. He hated jewelry. He wouldn't even wear his wedding ring most of the time."

"All right, well, I just thought I'd ask."

She held out her hand. "Just ... go on and give it to me."

"It's okay, Phoebe. I can get his jacket out of the evidence locker. It was insensitive of me to ask you to look at it."

"Give it here," she said. "I can handle it. I mean, I'm not sure I can, but I'd like to try for Lark's sake."

She snatched the photo out of my hand, flipped it around, and gasped. I tried taking it away from her, and she jerked it back.

"Give me a minute, sis," she said. "All right?"

"Okay."

She placed the photo on her lap, stared at it for a time, and ran a finger across Jack's face. She looked like she was about to cry, but she didn't.

"Where's the pin you're talking about?" she said. "I don't see it."

I leaned forward and pointed it out.

She furrowed her brow and looked closer. "I have no idea what it is. Couldn't it have come with the jacket? I mean, maybe it's the emblem of the brand of jacket he was wearing."

"Jack always dressed in Adidas when he wasn't at work, which is what he was wearing in this photo. You can see their trefoil logo on the upper left side. They don't have metal pins."

She shrugged and handed the photo back to me. "I have no idea what it is. Maybe it's a weird glare from the camera or something."

Maybe it was, and maybe it wasn't.

I needed to be sure.

P hoebe dropped me off at a storage unit I'd rented a couple of years before, right after my breakup with Liam. I removed the padlock, lifted the garage door, took the cover off the car, and stood back, inspecting my antique beauty. The tires looked good, and the car was remarkably clean for the length of time I'd neglected it, but a million-dollar question remained … Would it start?

The first few times I tried it sputtered and spit like a rebellious child cross with me for not giving it enough attention. It made sense. The car was in its eighties. I'd abandoned it. I hadn't kept up on its maintenance. It was one more nail in my coffin of guilt.

On the fourth attempt to fire it up, it hesitated and then growled back to life. I glanced at the time. I needed to get moving. But the car needed some TLC before it became my daily driver again. I drove it to the same repair place my Jeep had been towed to the night before, a shop I'd trusted for years. My timing was perfect. The Jeep had just been outfitted with new tires. I swapped one vehicle for the other and set off to make up for lost time.

An hour later, I tossed a tiny plastic bag onto a desk, pointed at it, and said, "What kind of pin do you think this is?"

Silas gloved up, removed the pin from the bag, and raised a brow. We exchanged glances, and he rubbed his fingers down his jawline, thinking.

"I mean, I don't know," he said. "It's worn, for starters. Whatever it was when it was first made, it's become something different now. What kind of pin do *you* think it is?"

"The symbol in the center almost looks like a rolled-up newspaper," I said, "but the metal is tarnished. It'll be hard to tell unless we get it polished."

"I have a better idea."

I followed Silas over to a microscope. He stuck the pin underneath it and took a look.

"See anything?" I asked.

"Yeah, see for yourself."

I bent down and peered through the magnifying lens. "It's not a rolled-up newspaper. It's a scroll with what looks to be a quill in front of it."

"I agree. Where'd you get it?"

"On Jack's jacket, the one he was wearing the night he was murdered. When you looked everything over, you missed this."

He swallowed—hard. "I ... uhh, can't believe ... I don't know how I— I mean, I kinda remember seeing it on the jacket, but I didn't think anything of it. I didn't see how it could be tied to his murder."

The difference between assumption and being thorough was a slippery slope, one he'd just slipped all the way down. It wasn't like him to make such an amateur mistake, but we were all guilty of them from time to time.

"Hey, it's okay," I said. "I should have noticed it too."

"Why's it so important?"

"I don't know. Maybe it isn't. I noticed it this morning in one of the crime scene photos, and I pointed it out to Phoebe. Jack wasn't into jewelry. She said he wouldn't have worn it."

It was a longshot to think something so insignificant could be the catalyst that would lead to the killer's undoing, but I was willing to follow any leads at this point. And if Jack didn't wear jewelry, why had he worn it that night?

38

There was one person I still hadn't interviewed yet—the elusive Mitch Porter. Today he'd have an audience with me whether he liked it or not. I pulled into Phoebe's driveway, parked, and walked across the street. Holly Porter saw me coming, waved at me through her front window, and met me at the door.

"I need to speak to Mitch," I said.

"Good morning to you too," she said.

"Is he here?"

"Not right now."

"He *does* live here, right? Because he never seems to be home."

"Of course, he lives here," she said. "He's just a busybody, and he's always running around. He likes to keep active."

"If it's easier for me to go to him, I can. Is he at work?"

She shook her head. "He popped out to the store for me. I was getting ready to make cookies, and wouldn't you know it, I realized I was out of butter. Well, not all the way out. I had a quarter cup, and I needed a half a cup, and he said he'd run out and get some for me, and—"

Please, woman.

Stop rambling about things no one else cares about.

I was starting to think she yammered just to hear the sound of her own voice.

"When do you expect him back?" I asked.

"I don't know. Fifteen minutes or so, if he comes straight back, that is. You all right, honey? You don't look good."

No, I wasn't all right.

I was frustrated and worried and stressed.

"I'm fine," I said.

She raised a brow. "Mmm … are you, though? You know, my mother came for a visit a couple of months ago. She struggles with anxiety and a bit of depression from time to time. Anyhoo, she left behind a bottle of herbal anxiety pills, and … well, I've never struggled with any of those things, and please don't take this the wrong way, I don't mean to offend, but it just seems to me like you are. I'd be happy to give you the bottle if you'd like."

I didn't know whether to thank her or deck her in her annoying, exuberant face.

"No thanks," I said. "I'm good."

"Suit yourself. If you change your mind, they'll be here."

A tender, young voice said, "Mommy?"

Holly turned. "Come here, Ethan. Say hello to Mommy's friend."

Ethan crept up and stood behind Holly, hiding part of his face behind her dress.

"Hi, Ethan," I said. "How are you doing today?"

He poked his head around her dress and blinked at me but said nothing.

"Don't be shy," Holly said. "She's nice. She's going to find Lark and bring her back so you can play with her again."

Great job, Holly.

Make promises you have no idea if you or I can keep.

Ethan looked at Holly. "Can I have a fruit snack?"

"You've already had one today, honey."

"Pleeeeease," Ethan said.

"It depends. What do you want more, fruit snacks or cookies? Because when Daddy gets home, I'll finish making the cookies, and you can't have both."

I was shocked. I didn't see her as a strict parent.

Ethan whined in dissatisfaction and sauntered back down the hallway, resigned to wait for the cookies she'd promised.

Once he was out of earshot, Holly said, "It's my fault, you know."

"What's your fault?" I asked.

"Ever since Lark's been missing, I've been spoiling him. He's having a hard time dealing with what happened to her. He has nightmares every night now, and he's started wetting the bed, which he's never done. He thinks since someone took her, they'll come back and take him. Before it happened, he was an outgoing, rambunctious kid. Now he's timid, afraid of his own shadow."

We internalized so much as adults, it was easy to forget what a child might be experiencing.

"I'm sorry," I said. "I can't imagine what Ethan must be going through."

"Lark was his best friend. The first day he met her, he told me when they grew up, they were going to get married. It was the sweetest thing he'd ever said. I pray for her every night. I just know you'll find her."

She had the kind of faith in me I should have had in myself but didn't.

"I need to head to Phoebe's house for a bit," I said. "I'll hang around there until Mitch gets home. Will you send him over when he gets back?"

She nodded. "You bet."

I crossed the street feeling an overwhelming rush of emotions. The weight of all those counting on me kept piling higher and higher. It had been too long. I needed to catch a break soon.

I entered Phoebe's house and tried to resist approaching the wall in the living room that Phoebe called "the wall of photos." I couldn't resist. Her hobby had always been taking photos of those she loved, framing them, and adding them to various walls in her home.

Phoebe's photo wall had amassed over ninety frames over time. Each photo captured was a cherished memory frozen in time—when life was breezy and the reality of the chaos of the present day was unimaginable. Now it had all changed.

I pressed my hand against the wall and hung my head, gasping for air.

"Detective," a male voice said. "You wanted to see me?"

I closed my eyes and attempted to force myself back to some sense of normal before I addressed him.

I glanced in his direction and said, "Are you Mitch Porter?"

He nodded.

"If I didn't know any better, I'd think you've been avoiding me," I said.

"Sorry, I've had a lot going on. I'd planned to contact you today."

I wasn't sure I believed it.

Mitch was handsome, in a rugged, rough-around-the-edges kind of way, a vast difference from the polished look of his wife. His long, dark hair had been fastened into a bun, and he sported a goatee that hadn't been spruced up in a couple of days. Phoebe had said Mitch and Jack golfed together, which, given his appearance at present, amazed me.

"Has anyone ever said you look like Leonardo DiCaprio?" I asked.

"Yeah, a few times. I'm not sure why. I don't see it."

"Your eyes and the shape of your face are similar."

He seemed unnerved by the compliment. But I hadn't elaborated on what I saw when I looked into his eyes. They were shifty.

"What can I do for you?" he asked.

I gazed at his shoes, a pair of dark blue Nikes.

"Nice footwear," I said. "Heard you're a size eleven."

"I am. What about it?"

"Forensics found a shoe print in Phoebe's back yard the night of the murder. Size ten. And Hattie thought she saw a man run past her house wearing Nike shoes right after she heard gunfire coming from Phoebe's house. Size ten isn't much different than size eleven."

"I was here the night Jack was killed, so even if the print is mine, it doesn't mean I had anything to do with what happened to him or to Lark."

"I never said you did."

He slid his hands inside his pockets and leaned against the wall. "Didn't you? Whatever you're thinking, why not just say it?"

Fine.

I will.

"Where were you last night?" I asked.

"Home, with my family."

"All night?"

"Yep. Talk to Holly. She'll verify it."

I didn't doubt it, but would she be telling the truth?

"I'll ask her," I said.

"Fine, anything else?"

"Yeah," I said. "Take off your shirt."

"What?"

My instructions had been clear.

"Your shirt. Take it off."

"Why?"

"Because I asked you to do it."

He crossed his arms in front of him. "I don't think so, no."

I jerked my gun out of the holster and pointed it at him.

He threw his hands in the air. "What the hell?"

"Take. Your. Shirt. Off. Mitch." I paused for effect and then added, "Please."

"You can't force me to remove my clothing."

"I'm not asking for a lap dance. I just need to take a quick look at your chest."

"What you're doing isn't okay. You can't just pull a gun on me."

"You know what Lark means to me, and to my sister," I said. "Do you think I give a shit about what's right and what isn't right at this point? I've given you a simple request, and the fact you're not accommodating it raises even more questions than I had before. Do what I ask, and I'll put the gun away."

"Man," he said. "Jack told me a while back that you kinda went off the deep end, but I never expected you to be this—"

"Stop talking."

"Why? Because I'm speaking the truth? You think because you have a badge, you can do whatever you want? You can't."

Take a breath, Georgiana.

Take a breath and think it through.

I took a breath.

Then I took another.

I felt no different.

I flashed back to a conversation I'd had with Harvey when I first became a detective. He'd said it would be a lot easier if I applied the sandwich rule when trying to get information out of people. His suggestion was to first offer the suspect a compliment. Second, in a casual, non-threatening way, tell the suspect what I needed to know and why. And third, end the request with a generic statement like, "Any information you could share with us would be great. We appreciate your help."

In my own experience, all the sandwich rule did was give guilty suspects the chance to appear innocent, and that wasn't a game I was willing to play. Holly was a perfect example. I was convinced part of her buttery-sweet persona was due to the fact she was gifted at the art of being fake-nice. But whether the level of fake was twenty percent or eighty, I didn't know. What I did know was that Harvey's advice was ringing so loud in my ears, it was like he was right there with me.

I angled the gun away from Mitch and said, "Last night I was ambushed inside of a private investigator's office downtown. It was too dark for me to get a good look at the man who shot at me, but I fired back, and he was hit. Before we go any further, I need to be certain that man wasn't you. If you take your shirt off, I'll have my answer."

Mitch paused for a moment and then said, "Good story. I'm still not taking my shirt off, though."

And there it was—a perfect example of why the sandwich rule didn't work for a person like me.

I raised the gun again, but this time, I pulled the trigger. The bullet whizzed past Mitch and lodged into the wall behind him.

"I can't believe it!" he said. "You shot at me!"

"I didn't shoot *at* you. I shot next to you. Now, get your shirt off before I become more annoyed than I already am."

For once, he didn't resist. He ripped his shirt off and thrust it to the ground.

"There!" he said. "Satisfied?"

Almost.

"Turn around."

He spread his hands to the side and turned, and I had my answer. There wasn't a single scratch on his gym-sculpted body.

"If you had nothing to hide," I said, "why didn't you take your shirt off the first time I asked?"

He opened his mouth to reply, and Hattie burst through the front door wielding the prize knife in her collection.

She looked at me, and then at a shirtless Mitch. She stared at his chest a bit longer than necessary and said, "What in heaven's name is going on?"

"Nothing," I said.

"Doesn't look like *nothing* to me," she said.

"We're fine, Hattie. I was just having a simple conversation with Mitch."

Hattie pointed the knife at the hole in the wall. "Simple, eh? Doesn't look simple to me. No siree. You better start talking."

"Hattie," Mitch said. "Call Chief Kennison. Tell him she pulled a gun on me and then shot at me."

Hattie squinted at me, debating his request, and then shifted her gaze to him. "She shot at you, eh? I'm looking right at you. I see no bullet wound."

"Yeah, well, she missed," he said.

"I don't think so," Hattie said. "I know you, Mitchell. And I like you. But you're a stubborn mule of a thing at times. I've heard the way you talk to your wife when you think no one is listening. You seem to forget the windows in your house are often open. If the detective shot at you, I suppose she had her reasons."

Mitch's jaw dropped open. He appeared too stunned to speak.

"Looks like you have everything under control here, Detective," Hattie said. "You're not going to kill him, right?"

"Of course not," I said.

"Well then, carry on." Hattie walked over to Mitch, picked his shirt off the ground, and handed it to him. "A bit of advice if I may, Mitchell. Drop the ego, stop your faffing, and help the detective find our girl."

39

Mitch sat in a chair across from me. He appeared less peeved than he had been a few minutes before, but it was clear he was not over what had just happened.

"Do you want a drink or anything?" I asked.

"I *want* to get back to my family," he said. "Tell me what I need to say in order to do that."

I wondered if he'd exact his revenge later by snitching on me over the gun incident. Another conversation with Mayor Wheeler was one I'd hoped to avoid, but I didn't regret my actions. And something about the tone in Hattie's voice when she spoke to Mitch about having eavesdropped on his conversations with Holly led me to believe whatever she'd heard wasn't major, but enough to convince him to keep his mouth shut about me stepping over the line.

"I'd like to talk to you about the night Jack was killed," I said.

"So, talk."

"Jack was wearing a lapel pin on his jacket. We've taken a closer look at it and now know the design is a scroll and quill. Any idea where he got it or why he was wearing it?"

He shrugged. "None."

"Phoebe said he never wore jewelry. Did you notice him wearing the pin when you visited him that night?"

"I don't know. I don't remember."

It seemed short answers were all I could expect from here on out, which meant I was wasting my time. Maybe he *couldn't* help me.

Someone knocked on the front door.

"Come in," I said.

Holly bounced down the hallway holding a plate of cookies in her hands. She slid them onto my lap and said, "These are for you!"

"I, ahh, thank you," I said.

She moved her hands to her hips. "So … how are things going here? You two almost done? I'm having trouble with the garbage disposal, and I need to steal Mitch away so he can take a look at it."

"We're done," I said, "for now."

"Hope he was able to help," she said.

"Can I ask you a question before you go, Holly?" I asked.

"You bet," she said.

"Was Jack wearing a lapel pin the night he was murdered?"

She tapped a finger to her lips, thinking. "You know, yeah, I think so. I didn't know what it was, so I asked him about it."

"What did he say?"

"He said it had been given to him by an old friend, someone he'd known a long time ago. I remember thinking it was strange because he'd never worn it before."

I looked at Mitch. "You said you don't remember if you saw it or not. Where were you when Holly's conversation with Jack took place?"

"I dunno," Mitch said.

"I was in the kitchen with Jack at the time, helping him grab some dishes and utensils for the food," Holly said. "I believe Mitch was outside with the kids."

"Did Jack say anything else?"

She shook her head. "Not about the pin, but while we were in the kitchen, he pulled up a music playlist on his phone and put on a Matchbox Twenty song. Hmm. I'm trying to remember the name of it."

"Unwell?"

She shook her head. "I think it was 'If You're Gone' ... yeah, that was it. He started humming the words to it and then he said the oddest thing."

"What did he say?"

"He asked me if there was ever anyone I loved before Mitch whom I considered to be the one who got away."

"Why did you find it odd?"

"Because Jack didn't talk much about personal things. It was obvious the song meant something to him. I was sure he was thinking of someone else—someone other than Phoebe."

"What did you say?"

Holly craned her head and noticed Mitch hanging on to her every word.

"I said no, of course," she said. "I've never loved anyone the way I love my husband."

Her eyes said something else, but with Mitch sitting in the same room, I forgave the lie.

"What else did you two talk about?" I asked.

"I asked him the same question. He didn't answer at first. It was like his mind was somewhere else. Then he said we'd better start eating before the food got cold, so the discussion ended."

Mitch and Holly left the house, and I remained, thinking about what she'd just said. I did a search and found it was the sixth most popular song on the Billboard music charts in 2001, which also happened to be the same year Jack graduated.

I assumed Jack was thinking about an old high school flame when he posed the question to Holly. I walked to his home office and scanned his bookshelves. On the far left, beneath a decorative candle, were Jack's old yearbooks. I took them to his desk, sat down, and opened his freshman one. I flipped through its pages and found nothing of real significance. The written messages left by other girls were innocent and funny. There was nothing to suggest he'd had a romantic attachment of any kind.

I moved onto his sophomore yearbook. It offered little more information than the first one had. Jack was a model student. He was well-liked by everyone. He played on the junior varsity football team and was on student council. He was the proverbial boy next door.

Jack's yearbook for his junior year took a turn I hadn't expected when I came upon a group photo of Jack and several other classmates. It was the yearbook club photo. Jack had his arm draped around a girl. I checked the caption for the photo and found her name: Rebecca Martin. The fact he was cozy with her wasn't what stood out the most, though. It was the matching lapel pins every student in the group had attached to their shirts, pins that looked just like the one I'd analyzed that morning.

I flipped to the back of the book and searched the name Rebecca Martin and then looked through the photos attached to it. In the football section, I came across a photo of Rebecca in a cheerleading uniform arm-in-arm with Jack at a football game. A heart had been drawn around the photo with a blue ink pen, and next to it the words "R+J forever" were written in cursive.

Was Rebecca the one he'd referred to when listening to the song playing on the night of his death? Why was he so nostalgic about it? Could she have been the person he'd hired the PI to find?

I set the first three yearbooks to the side and reached for the last one. I opened it and an envelope slipped out. I reached down, picked it up, and removed the folded letter tucked inside.

Dear Jack,

I'm sure it comes as a surprise to you to hear from me after all these years. The truth is I've thought of you many times over the years, and I've often wondered where you ended up after high school. I know you were upset when I made the abrupt decision to move away and then asked my parents not to give you my contact information. I was young and still reeling over the last discussion we'd had right after you started college. It's been so long ago now, you may not even remember what was said, but it was a conversation I'll never forget.

I remember thinking when you picked me up that night that you'd come home from college to propose. In my mind, it made sense. You took me to the nicest restaurant in the city, gave me a bouquet of roses, and showered me with compliments. You told me you missed me. You told me you missed being home. You told me how much I'd love college next year after I graduated. I was so happy I didn't realize that for everything you'd said, there were things you hadn't. All I could focus on were the images swirling around in my head of the life we'd have together. But I couldn't have been more wrong.

When you dropped me off at home that night, I leaned in for a kiss, and you said, "Becca, wait. There's something I need to tell you." You said you would always love me, but you were in college now, and you wanted to be free—free to date other girls and hang out with friends on the weekends, which you weren't able to do since you'd been coming home to see me. My tears and heartfelt sentiments about how good we were together weren't enough to sway you. I'll never forget getting out of the car and hearing Matchbox Twenty playing in the background. You put your window down and tried to console me by saying after I graduated and joined you at school, if we were both single, maybe we could pick up where we left off.

To this day, I don't understand when you decided I was a weak enough person to have entertained the idea of a reconciliation after you ripped my heart out. But for the first time, I saw you as you saw me instead of the way I'd always imagined you had. Bitter and broken, I learned weeks later of your relationship with my replacement, a girl named Phoebe. I moved to San Francisco and vowed never to speak to you again.

I'm sure you're wondering why I've decided to dredge up the past after so long. It's time you knew the truth. And I hope you'll understand why I chose to do what I did.

The last night we were together, when we had sex in the back seat of your father's car before you took me home, I got pregnant. I thought about telling you, but I didn't because I know you, and I knew you'd do what you considered to be the "right thing." You would have dropped out of school, you would have married me, and I would have spent my life wondering if you loved me or if you just did what you felt you had to do. I deserved better. I deserved someone who loved me for me. Our baby did too.

You have a daughter. Her name is Maya. She's eighteen years old. She graduated this year and has a scholarship to Stanford University. She's smart, funny, has the same drive you always had in school, and when I look at her, she reminds me more of you than myself. She has your eyes.

I'm sorry I didn't tell you about her before. I should have, and the truth is, she doesn't know she has a different father than the one she's known all her life. If you can find it in your heart to forgive me, I would like to see you. Maybe we can ease her in, and after a few visits, we can tell her together. She's an adult now, and I believe she'd want to know.

If you have no interest in being in her life or mine, I understand. The choice is yours. Before I offer my phone number and address, I'd like to ask you to respond by sending me a letter in the mail first. I know it seems like an archaic way of communicating, but for now, it's the most discreet way for both of us.

I hope wherever you are in life, you are happy, and I await your reply.

Rebecca

Rebecca Martin
PO Box 51997
Santa Barbara, CA 93101

P.S. I was searching through boxes the other day and came across the pin I received in our yearbook class. I wondered if you still had yours. If not, I've sent it along as an example of a fond memory we shared in better times.

I know why Jack hired a private investigator," I said.

Phoebe poured a glass of water, sat down, and craned her neck to the side, searching the back yard for our mother who was still outside chatting with the next-door neighbor.

"Oh…kay," Phoebe said. "You better get to it. Once Mom sees you're here, she'll rush back inside."

"It's just … what I'm about to say will be a shock, Phoebe."

"With all that's happened, I don't think I can be any more surprised than I already am."

She was wrong.

"A long time ago, Jack had a child with someone else," I said. "A girl."

"He … whaaaat?"

"Her name is Maya. She's eighteen. I assume you don't know about her?"

She shook her head. "If I had known, I would have told you."

"I hoped maybe he'd told you."

"You're saying he *knew* about her? I don't understand. Why would he find out he had a kid and never say anything to me?"

I didn't know.

I guessed he'd hired a private investigator to make sure Rebecca was telling the truth first.

"I checked the postmark on the envelope. Jack didn't know about Maya until about a month ago."

Phoebe waved a hand in front of her. "Wait a minute. How do you know this?"

"It will make more sense if I show you," I said.

I pulled the letter out of my bag and handed it to her. Phoebe pored over it, her eyes flickering with various emotions as she read through to the end. Once she finished, she folded it back up and tossed it across the table.

"Wow," she said. "I mean, I've read the letter now, and I still don't want to believe it."

"Did Jack ever talk to you about Rebecca?"

"A few times. He shared some experiences they'd had in high school. The way he talked about her, I took it she was nothing more than a crush."

I considered telling her about the comment Jack had made to Holly the night he died, but I decided not to bring it up. Jack was dead. Whether or not he'd rekindled an old flame no longer mattered. It didn't seem right to tarnish his memory with my own speculations.

"I'm sure you're right," I said. "If he wanted to be with her, he would have been. Instead, he broke things off, and the two of you met and fell in love."

"It's weird to think about him having a child with someone else," she said. "He wasn't against kids, but after we got married, I wanted to try right away. He convinced me to wait. He wanted us to make our own memories together before we had kids. All that time, he already had a child and didn't even know it."

"Andy Sanders was killed because of something he found out that the killer didn't want anyone else to know. I need to track down Jack's ex. Once I do, we'll find Lark. I'm sure of it."

"I hope you're right."

I eyed my mother. She'd taken a few steps back from the fence, which meant her conversation was about to wrap up. I needed to take my leave before she came in and found a reason to keep me any longer.

"Before Jack died, did he take any trips out of town?" I asked.

Phoebe tapped a finger on the table, thinking. "I don't think so. Not overnight."

According to the letter, Rebecca Martin lived in Santa Barbara, about one hundred thirty miles away from Cambria. Jack could have skipped out on work one morning and driven to see Rebecca. If he timed it right, and avoided rush-hour traffic, he could have gone there and back in a day.

Rebecca's letter had been sent to Jack's work address, which was why Phoebe never knew it existed. I wondered if Jack had replied to Rebecca's letter and whether or not they'd met. If they had, what had their conversation been like? Had he met Maya, or had Rebecca held off on the introductions like she'd suggested doing in the letter?

I had more questions than answers, but for the first time, I was certain I was close to finding Lark.

41

I dropped Luka off at Aunt Laura's house, gave him a big squeeze, and promised her I wouldn't be gone longer than needed. She shrugged and told me not to worry—Luka was always welcome. Aunt Laura loved me, even more than she loved my siblings, I suspected, but ever since I'd adopted Luka, I was convinced she loved him even more. I didn't blame her. I loved him more than I loved most humans too.

I arrived in Santa Barbara at dusk and headed straight for Rebecca Martin's last known address. She lived in Montecito, considered one of the best suburbs in the area, and even though the condo she lived in seemed small from the outside, I was sure its price tag exceeded the million-dollar mark.

Rebecca's place was an end unit located on the bottom floor. The lights were out when I arrived. It didn't seem late enough for her to have retired to bed. Perhaps she wasn't home. I decided to find out.

I knocked on the door. No one answered, and I heard no one stirring inside. I knocked again. Still nothing. I exercised four minutes of patience. I thought about exercising more. The idea didn't appeal to me, so I walked around the back side of the house and hopped over the short wooden fence, pleased to find the back door wasn't secured by a dead bolt. I made excellent use of a hairpin and showed myself inside.

"Hello?" I said. "Is anyone home?"

Not wanting to alarm Rebecca's neighbors who might know she was away, I kept the interior lights off and resorted to a small flashlight I had in my pocket. The condo was a single level with three rooms. I checked out the master first. The bed had been left unmade and unfolded laundry was strewn all over it. None of the wrinkled clothes on the bed were for a woman. They were all for a man.

I walked to the closet and found it full of clothes, shoes, and accessories belonging to both a woman and a man. I assumed the man's items could have belonged to Rebecca's husband, if she had one, or a boyfriend who lived with her. Whomever he was, it was clear they shared the house.

I entered the second bedroom and aimed the flashlight at the wall above the bed. The name MAYA was at the top of a bulletin board in thin, pink, wooden block letters. Beneath it were photos of Maya and her friends, and I discovered she was or had been a cheerleader in school just like her mother.

Maya was an attractive young woman. She was tall and slender with long, blond hair, and she had a kind, crooked smile that reminded me of Jack. The resemblance to him was obvious. I was convinced she was who Rebecca claimed. Most of the clothes in Maya's closet had been removed, which told me she didn't live there anymore. Given her age, it was possible she'd gone off to college already or lived on her own.

The third room contained two desks, one on each side. The desk on the left was neat and tidy, and its minimal contents had all been positioned with perfect precision. There was a framed photo to the right that appeared to be Maya and Rebecca. Maya was dressed in a high school graduation cap and gown, and Rebecca beamed with pride like any proud mother would.

The desk on the right was littered with paper, pens, and a few bowls which had once contained food and were now empty, for the most part. A bible found in the top drawer was inscribed with the name Anthony. It was dusty, like it hadn't been removed from the drawer since it had been placed there.

I left the bedroom and walked to the living area, surprised to find it almost devoid of furniture. There were no sofa or chairs, and the walls were barren. All that remained was a television resting on the floor on top of a diamond-patterned blue-and-white rug.

The kitchen wasn't much different than the living room. A few of the cupboards had been left open, but there was nothing inside. Several flat moving boxes rested on the kitchen counter and next to them, a roll of packing tape. It appeared the residents of the home were moving, but when, and where, and why had they decided to do it? Even more pressing … where were they now?

A strange feeling of emptiness overcame me, a heaviness I couldn't shake. Something was amiss, and yet, I wasn't certain what it was. It was like one day they were here, and the next they'd all vanished.

42

The following morning, I drove by Rebecca's house again. It was the same as it had been the night before—deserted. Where was everyone?

I called Harvey and checked in. He'd been in contact with the police departments in the surrounding counties to let them know I was in the area following up on an investigation. I then called Hunter, whom I'd texted the night before. She'd done some digging for me and learned Rebecca had gotten married in 2002, which meant Maya had been two years old at that time. Rebecca had also chosen to keep her maiden name and had not taken on her husband's surname: Paine. Hunter had located the name and address of Rebecca's parents, Stuart and Judith Martin. They lived in Carpinteria, a short drive from where I was now.

I arrived at the gate of the Martins' home soon after and found an enormous house with sweeping views of the ocean. It was the kind of house I imagined was equipped with a butler, maids, and gardeners to tend to the daily upkeep of the place.

I pulled up to the front gate and pressed the buzzer.

Seconds later a pleasant female voice said, "Can I help you?"

"Yes," I said. "I'm looking for Stuart and Judith Martin."

"I'm Judith," she said, "but everyone calls me Judy. Who are you, and why are you here?"

"My name is Georgiana Germaine. I'm a detective in San Luis Obispo. I wanted to ask you a few questions about a case I'm working on."

"All right. I'll buzz you in and meet you outside."

I entered the driveway slow enough to admire the many hours that had gone into the gardens, which offered a meticulous, picturesque display of color. In a small way, it reminded me of my own garden, the one I'd had when I was married to Liam. He hadn't kept it up after I'd left and now it was dead, much like our marriage. Taking in my current surroundings, the desire to dig my hands into the soil and garden again appealed to me. Maybe it was time to consider setting down roots.

I pulled the Jeep up to the front of the house and got out. Judith walked toward me, raising a brow as she examined my Jeep and then the sparkling-white power-washed pavement it was parked on.

"Don't worry," I said. "I know it's old, but it doesn't leak oil or anything."

She folded her arms and narrowed her eyes, which meant my assurance wasn't enough to sway her opinion.

"How can you be sure?" she asked.

"I would know if it did. If it makes you feel better, I can park it on the street."

"Would you mind?" she asked.

"Not at all."

"Why don't you drive out past the gate, and we can talk there?"

I complied with her request, waiting as she disappeared back inside her house to grab a floppy beach hat before walking down to meet me. Judy was impressive for her age. I guessed she was around seventy, even though she looked at least ten years younger. She was slender, toned and stylish, wearing an oversized pair of black Audrey Hepburn-style sunglasses and a white, fitted sundress.

"What do I have to do with the case you're working on?" she asked.

"I'm trying to find your daughter," I said.

"Which one? I have five."

"Rebecca."

At the mention of Rebecca's name, I noted a swift shift in Judy's otherwise pleasant demeanor. Her face had soured. I wondered why.

"What do you want with Rebecca?"

"Do you remember Jack Donovan, a boy she dated in high school?"

"Of course, I remember Jack. He came to our house all the time … well, until he ran off to college. Nice boy."

"The breakup was hard on Rebecca, wasn't it?"

"I don't suppose it was much different than any other break-up kids go through when they suffer the pain of losing their first love. It hurts, but after some time passes, they get over it."

"Rebecca thought Jack would marry her one day, didn't she?"

"She did. But she was too young to know who she was or what she wanted yet. She thought her world was over if she couldn't be with Jack, but she got over him. Why are you here, asking me these questions?"

"Jack Donovan was my brother-in-law. He was married to my sister Phoebe."

We locked eyes and stood there for a time, staring at one another in silence. She was thinking, contemplating what to say next versus what she thought she shouldn't say.

"I saw it on the news," she said. "Couldn't believe it when I heard. I'm sorry. My deepest condolences to your family. Did you find out who killed him?"

"Not yet, but I'm close."

"What about your niece? I forget her name. Lara?"

"Lark."

"That's right. Any word on her whereabouts?"

I shook my head.

"Your family is going through hell right now," she said. "I feel for you all."

The sentiment seemed genuine, like one she had experienced herself. And while it had been nice talking with her, it was taking too much time. I pulled the letter Rebecca had written out of my bag and held it in front of her.

"What is it?" she asked.

"Rebecca wrote a letter to Jack. She told him Maya was his daughter. She invited him to drive up to Montecito and meet her. I'm trying to find your daughter so I can talk to her about it. I need to know if Jack met with her and what happened when he did."

The sound of women's voices echoed from behind. Judith craned her neck, smiling at two women walking on the sidewalk in our direction. Both women were dressed in track suits and baseball caps and appeared to be power walking. The woman in the gray track suit caught sight of Judith, and her eyes widened as she rushed over to her.

"Oh, my goodness, Judy!" she said. "It's nice to see you out of the house. We were just talking about how much we've missed you."

Gray Track Suit pointed at Lavender Track Suit and said, "Sally was just saying she hoped you'd decide to start walking with us again, and I agree."

"Soon," Judy said. "I promise."

Gray Track Suit and Lavender Track Suit exchanged glances as if they knew they'd stumbled into the middle of a conversation they weren't meant to be part of, and although it was obvious they wanted to stay, they seemed well aware we wouldn't continue our discussion if they did.

"We'll be on our way," Lavender Track Suit said. "We're here for you whenever you're ready. Just give us a call."

Judy assured them she would, and the women waved goodbye and kept moving, leaving me to wonder why Judy used to join them for walks but no longer did. She didn't appear to have any injuries preventing her from daily exercise, and I could tell she missed them as much as they missed her.

Once the women were a fair distance away, Judy said, "Why don't we continue this conversation inside?"

"I was hoping to get Rebecca's phone number," I said. "I need to talk with her."

Judy shook her head. "It's not possible."

"Why not?"

"Because … my daughter is dead."

43

Rebecca was dead.

I didn't want it to be true.

But it was true, and I had to accept it.

I was sitting on an expensive yet uncomfortable turquoise, velvet chair in Judy's sitting room, staring at a thirty-foot-high waterfall feature cascading down the wall. It was ridiculous and grandiose, but I couldn't tear my eyes away from it. It was soothing, making me forget for a moment where I was and why I was there.

Judy entered the room carrying a cheese plate like a waitress carrying a tray of food to a table at a restaurant. She set the spread down on the coffee table in front of me and said, "Eat some of this, would you? My neighbors keep bringing food dishes over, even though I've told them to stop. Stuart doesn't even like cheese, and I can't eat all of this myself."

Not one to turn down quality cheese of any kind, I sliced into a chunk of brie, pasted it onto a multi-grain cracker, and popped it into my mouth.

"I didn't know Rebecca had died," I said. "How long ago?"

"She passed eighteen days ago. It's hard, you know. Some days, two weeks feels like a year. Others, it feels like I just saw her yesterday."

I knew the feeling.

"What happened?" I asked.

"Breast cancer. I'll never forget the day she found out. I couldn't believe it. I thought we'd get through it, that she would get better, but by the time she was diagnosed, it didn't matter what we did or how much money was spent fighting it. There wasn't anything any of us could do to save her."

"I'm sorry."

"Me too."

"Rebecca grew up here, didn't she, in Carpinteria?"

"She did. Right here in this house."

"How did she keep Maya a secret from those who knew her for so long?"

"Before anyone could spot a baby bump, we sent her to my sister's house in San Francisco. She loved it there. We bought her a house, and we flew to see her two or three times a month. She didn't return to Carpinteria until Maya was five. By then, she was married to Anthony, and he'd been in the picture long enough for everyone to assume Maya was his daughter."

"What can you tell me about Anthony?"

"We didn't like him at first."

"Why not?"

"I suppose we turned our noses up at him. We live a privileged life, and we wanted Rebecca to marry well."

"By 'well,' you mean upper class?"

"Yes. Anthony came from a rather poor upbringing. His mother was a maid, and his father was a truck driver before he died. They saved almost every penny they earned to put Anthony through school, and he used his degree to start his own business. A successful business, I might add."

"What made you change your mind about him?" I asked.

"The way he loved our daughter, and because he accepted Maya as his own. As much as we didn't want to approve of their union, we came to love him in time."

"Did you know about the letter Rebecca wrote Jack?"

Judy sat on the chair opposite me and clasped her hands together on her lap. "I did. I was the one who convinced her to write it. I knew the secret she'd kept had taken a toll on her over the years. I thought Jack had a right to know the truth and that she needed to free herself from the lie before she passed."

"Were you aware Jack hired a private investigator?"

She nodded. "After he received the letter she wrote, Rebecca didn't hear back from Jack for a couple of weeks. A short time later, we found out he'd hired a private investigator to verify if there was any merit to what she'd told him."

"And did he get the confirmation he needed?"

"He did, in the end. The private investigator provided him with her birth certificate. The date matched up with the last time Jack and Rebecca had seen each other. Even so, Jack still questioned it. He told the PI he wanted to get a court order for a DNA test, but once the private investigator showed him the photos he'd taken of Maya, Jack knew she was his."

"How do you know all of this?"

"Once Jack believed he was Maya's biological father, he sent Rebecca a letter, explaining why he'd taken so long to reply, and he asked if they could meet."

"I'm guessing they did. How did it go?"

"He was agitated at first. I expect he'd brooded over the fact she'd kept Maya from him all those years and he planned to give her a piece of his mind. When he arrived, he learned Rebecca was not long for this world, and his demeanor changed. Rebecca asked for forgiveness, and after a long conversation, they made amends."

"Then what happened?"

"Rebecca wanted Jack to meet Maya, but she worried about how to go about it. There was no way to spare her from the pain the truth would cause, but Rebecca thought it would help if they eased in. Her solution was to invite Jack to Maya's upcoming birthday party. She planned on telling Maya he was an old friend from high school who had stopped by to see her because he'd heard she was ill."

"And then what?"

"Rebecca asked Jack to find a way to strike up a casual conversation with Maya while he was there. But she asked him not to reveal who he was that night. She thought it best if they saw each other a few times first."

"Anthony raised Maya from the time she was a toddler," I said. "He was the only father she'd ever known. What did he have to say about it all?"

"It was hard on him at first. He adores her. But he understood Rebecca's desire to end her life with a clear conscience."

Judy sighed like she needed a diversion from the weight of our conversation. She leaned forward and scooted the cheese plate toward me.

"Have a bit more, won't you?" she asked.

I didn't want to confess I'd passed a McDonald's on my way over and allowed myself one of my favorite indulgences, a Sausage McMuffin with Egg.

"I had a lot to eat this morning. Sorry."

"Don't be. I'll wrap it up, and you can take it with you."

"I appreciate the—"

She huffed an abrasive sound of displeasure. "Nonsense. If you don't take it, it will end up in the trash. You decide."

Was it *my* decision, though?

I felt compelled to accept the offering whether I wanted to or not. The various cheeses on the platter looked like they had a good week or two before they'd start to become questionable. I despised frivolous waste, so I resigned myself to the fact I was about to be the proud new owner of an appetizer tray I didn't really want.

A restless irritation rose inside me, pulsing through me like I'd shot myself up with adrenaline. I'd spent the last several minutes trying to steer the conversation in the direction I wanted it to go, and in a single moment, it had disintegrated into a ridiculous exchange about cheese.

"I'll take the cheese," I said.

"Wonderful."

"Tell me about Maya's birthday party."

"Of course. Jack arrived early, and Rebecca introduced him to Maya. A while later, I found them sitting together at the table. Jack was talking about some of the memories he'd shared with Rebecca when they were in school. Knowing her mother's condition, it was the perfect icebreaker. She clung to his every word."

"Did Jack see Rebecca again—after the party?"

Judy squeezed her eyes shut and breathed as if she struggled to catch her breath. "A couple of nights after Maya's party, Rebecca's condition worsened, which was unexpected. We thought we had several weeks left with her. We didn't. She passed four days later."

"And Jack? Have you seen him since?"

"I texted him about Rebecca. He came to the funeral, and a few days later, he showed up here, looking for Maya."

"Did he see her?" I asked.

"Not to my knowledge. After the funeral, Anthony took her to Malaysia."

"Why Malaysia?"

"They'd taken a family vacation there a few years before. Rebecca loved it. She'd wanted to go back, but they never got the chance. They went there to scatter her ashes over the ocean."

"When did they return?"

Judy crossed one leg over the other. "Let's see now. I suppose they would have returned a little over a week ago."

The timeline fit.

"Did you tell Anthony that Jack was looking for Maya?" I asked.

"I did."

"What did he say?"

"Not much, though he did ask me where Jack lived."

"Why?"

"I don't know. He didn't say."

"Where is Maya now?"

"In school. The new semester just started. I suggested she take some time off, given what's just happened, but she said her mother would have wanted her to keep going, and she's right."

"What about Anthony? When's the last time you heard from him?"

"I haven't spoken to him since the conversation we had right after he got back. I tried calling a few times. He hasn't called back. I think he needs time to process what's happened. It's understandable. We all do."

"I've been to his house. No one was there."

She shrugged. "That's odd. Where else would he be?"

"What does Anthony do for work?" I asked.

"He's self-employed. He runs an online marketing business from home."

"After Rebecca died, did you consider telling Maya about Jack?"

"I did. I talked it over with Stuart, my husband. We were in two minds about it. Stuart thought we should hold off. I didn't. Jack has always been a persistent fellow. I knew he'd find a way to have Maya in his life, so I sent Anthony a text message to get his thoughts on the matter."

"When was this?" I asked.

"Right before he went off to Malaysia."

"What was Anthony's response to your message?"

"I can't remember the exact wording he used," she said. "Wait just a moment. I'll get my phone."

Either Judy was making light of her own suspicions or she lacked the skill of connecting the dots. In my own mind, the connection had been made, and my heart was racing.

Judy returned to the sitting room, squinting at her phone through a pair of bifocals.

"Here it is," she said. "Anthony thought Maya needed more time to adjust to life without her mother first, and he asked us to give it to her."

Of course, he did.

Her time to heal was his time to kill.

"Is there anywhere Anthony might stay other than his own house?" I asked.

"You could try his mother. She might know."

"Does she live around here?"

"She lives in Downey."

Downey.

Ninety-five miles from where I was now, but a mere seventeen miles from Cambria.

"How can I reach her?" I asked.

"I'll give you her address."

She scooped up the cheese platter and disappeared around the corner, returning a couple of minutes later. She handed me the platter, which she'd wrapped in cellophane. A yellow Post-it note with a handwritten address was stuck to the top. In an attempt to get going, I smiled and accepted the offering without hesitation.

"I'd like to show you something before I go," I said.

While she'd been in the kitchen, I'd queued up the photo and was ready to roll with it. I flipped my phone around and held it in front of her.

"Do you recognize this?" I asked.

She bent down, staring at the photo in question.

"Yes, I believe that's the money clip Rebecca gave Anthony on their tenth wedding anniversary."

To TP with love.

Anthony was short for Tony.

TP stood for Tony Paine.

I swallowed in an attempt to quell my tears.

The moment I'd been waiting for had come.

I had my man.

On the drive to Downey, I called Harvey and filled him in. I let him know I was headed to Anthony's mother's place, and he said he'd meet me there. I figured he might, which was why I'd waited to call him until I had almost reached my destination. I wanted to get there first.

Anthony's mother lived in a mint-colored, stucco house that looked like it had been built in the '30s and hadn't seen an ounce of renovation or upkeep since. The asphalt driveway was oil-stained and cracked, and the lawn had passed away several years earlier. It seemed Rebecca and Anthony had grown up in two different worlds, and yet somehow, they'd still ended up together.

I walked to the door and knocked. A slat in the cheap, metal miniblinds was lifted, and an eyeball peeked out. I waved at the eyeball, knocked again, and waited.

The front door opened a crack, just enough for the security chain to remain secure. A thin woman with a mound of dark, frizzy hair, and wearing cutoff jeans and a tank top, looked me in the eye and said, "Sorry, hun. No solicitors."

"I'm a detective," I said. "I need to talk to you about your son."

"He doesn't live here."

"I didn't ask if he lived here."

"Well, he don't, so there's nothing to say."

Bad grammar aside, I pushed harder.

"Where is he?" I asked.

She shrugged. "I don't know. At home, I suppose."

"When's the last time you saw him?"

"On the day of his wife's funeral."

"What kind of vehicle does he drive?"

"Why are you asking?"

"Why won't you just tell me?" I asked.

"Because I don't see how it's any of your business."

"Let me guess, then. A truck. Dark in color. Broken windshield. Am I right?"

She seemed unsure of how to respond, so she didn't.

"Are you married?" I asked. "Do you live here with anyone else?"

She shook her head. "It's just me. I already told you my son's not here. I'd like you to leave."

"I'd like you to let me in so we can continue this conversation."

"There's nothin' to talk about."

Inside the house, I heard a low, faint whine.

"What was that?" I asked.

"What was what?"

"The sound I heard coming from inside your house."

"I didn't hear anything."

I waited in silence and heard the sound again.

"You're not alone," I said. "Who else is here?"

The woman's eyes widened as she searched her mind for a sufficient answer. "Oh, I know what it is. It must be my cat. She's getting on in years, and she's always whining about something or other. I've thought about putting her down, but I've had her for so long I can't bring myself to do it."

It seemed the woman of few words could talk after all, long enough to make up a bogus story, at least. Whatever I'd heard, it wasn't a cat.

"Can I see it?" I asked.

"See what?"

"Your cat."

"She's resting now. You can't see her."

Every part of me screamed that something was awry.

I leaned forward until my face was a few inches from the crack in the doorway. "I've played nice, and I've tried to be polite. Wouldn't you agree?"

"I don't understand."

"I'm going to give you one chance. Got it? Not three, not five, *one*."

"One chance to what?"

"You're lying. Tell me the truth, or I'll bust this door down."

She tossed her head back and laughed. "You can't do anything. You're not allowed to because you'd get in trouble if you did. Screw you."

Screw me?

She turned, intending to close the door. I stepped back, lifted my foot, and drove it into the door. The chain busted loose, and the door opened, smacking her in the face. She stumbled backward and tumbled to the ground.

I showed myself inside, leaned over her trembling body, and said, "If you want the chain to work, invest in a better door next time, and never, ever turn your back on someone trying to get inside your house."

I glanced around and found the interior in far better condition than the exterior. The furniture was dated and sparse, but well-kept, and on prominent display was a lighted antique hutch filled with miniature crystal figurines.

"Where is he?" I asked. "Don't lie to me this time."

"I told you. I don't know."

"Where's Lark?"

"Who?"

"Lark Donovan, the little girl your son kidnapped the night he murdered my sister's husband."

The connection between who I was and why I was there and the personal connection I had to the case caused her to gasp and cover her mouth with her hand.

"Get up!" I said.

She averted her eyes but did what I asked.

I opened the door to my left. It was a small half-bath, with bars on the outside of the window to prevent a person from breaking in, or in my case, to prevent a person from breaking out.

"Get in there," I said.

"What? Why?"

"Do it."

She stepped inside. I slammed the door closed and grabbed a nearby chair. I jammed it against the doorknob, wedging it beneath the knob at an angle. It wouldn't hold her for long if she tried to get out, but I hoped it would hold her for long enough.

"Please don't do this," she said. "You don't understand."

She began sobbing.

"Stop crying," I said. "I need to look around, and I'll let you out in a few minutes."

"He's my son. Can't you understand? What would you expect me to do—turn on him? What kind of mother would I be if I had?"

An honest one, for starters.

I tore down the hallway toward the sound I'd heard before.

"Lark!" I screamed. "Are you here? It's Aunt Gigi. Talk to me."

Please let the voice I heard be hers.

Please.

Please.

Please.

The knob on the door at the end of the hall twisted open. Not knowing what to expect, I backed against the wall and readied my gun. The door creaked open, and a child stuck his head out. I squinted, staring at him for a moment, and realized the him wasn't a *him* at all. It was a *her*.

Her hair had been dyed, hacked off into a short crew cut, and she was dressed in a blue T-shirt with orange dinosaurs on it. Even so, there was no mistaking her.

I'd found her.

She was alive.

"It's okay, sweetheart," I said. "You're safe now. I'll take you to Mommy."

Lark stood in the doorway, blinking at me, frozen in place, confused.

I dropped to my knees and spread my arms. "Come here, baby girl. It's all right. I got you."

Lark burst into tears and rushed toward me, wrapping her arms around my neck. I showered her with kisses, promising never to walk out of her life again.

I felt someone tap my shoulder, and I swung around.

"Hey, are you okay?" Hunter asked.

"Yeah, where's Harvey?"

"In the other room, talking to the woman you locked in the bathroom." Hunter tipped her head toward Lark. "Is this … your niece?"

"Yeah," I said. "Yeah, it is."

Hunter smiled at me, and I nodded back, our eyes filling with tears.

"It's nice to meet you, Lark," Hunter said. "I'm Lilia. Lilia Hunter."

Lark, who still clung to me, buried her head into my chest.

"I … ahh … think I'll go and see if I can take over for Harvey so he can join you," Hunter said.

She walked away, and a minute later, Harvey rounded the corner. He clapped his hands together and said, "Where's Papa's favorite girl?"

Upon hearing his voice, Lark looked up, and shouted, "Papa!" She ran to him, and they embraced.

I patted him on the shoulder, leaned over his ear, and whispered, "I still don't know where Anthony is. You keep her, and I'll search the rest of the house."

"He could be anywhere," Harvey said. "Take Hunter with you."

I nodded and walked to the front room. Hunter was doing her best to reason with Anthony's frantic mother, who lurched out and clasped my arm when she saw me.

"I want you to know, I took care of her," she said. "I fed her and kept her clean. I read to her every night."

I jerked free from her grip. "I'll tell you what you did. You kept a child away from her mother, and then you took that child and tried to turn her into a boy so no one would recognize her. You didn't *care* for her. You *cared* for your son. Now you'll suffer the consequences of those actions, and I'll make sure I'm there to see it."

Harvey may have wanted Hunter to assist me, but Anthony's mother couldn't be left alone, and I didn't need or want the backup.

I searched the rest of the rooms in the house and came up empty. But there were signs he'd been staying there. Men's clothes had been folded into a drawer, shaving cream was on the countertop in the bathroom, and a laptop under the pillow in the guest room had a company logo sticker on it that read: *Paine-Free Marketing.*

Out of the bedroom window, a series of tarps caught my eye. They were covering something big. It wasn't hard to figure out what they were hiding.

45

heard a faint, rustling sound coming from beneath the tarps as I walked over, and given the air was still, I hoped I'd located Anthony. I reached out and ripped the edge of the first tarp back, eyeballing the truck that had almost mowed me down two nights before. I walked to the opposite side and yanked the second tarp free. I leaned against the glass and peered inside the cab. Aside from a fast-food bag and some loose change, it was empty.

Two tarps down, one to go.

I moved to the back of the truck, pausing a moment before the final reveal.

"Anthony Paine," I said, "if you want a Paine-Free arrest, this is your one chance to come out. Or don't. I'd be happy to extend you the same courtesy you gave Jack."

I eased the tarp away and flipped it on its side. A cat leapt off the back of the truck and scurried out of the yard. I stood there a moment, pressed a hand to my chest, and breathed, trying to slow my heart rate down.

What do you know?

Anthony's mother may not have lied about the cat after all.

I heard the sound of rustling beneath me, and I looked down. A hand reached out from beneath the truck, wrapped around my ankle, and yanked me back. I lost my footing and fell to the ground. My gun flew out of my hand, landing several feet away from me.

I reached for it, and Anthony grabbed for my other leg. I cracked my foot onto his head and backed toward the gun. He crawled out from under the truck, dragged me toward him, and drove his fist into my face. I lay there for a moment, my eye throbbing, eyes boring into his as he attempted to pin me down and finish what he'd started.

I pressed my knee into his stomach to stop him from moving forward, kicked his hip with my foot, grabbed his ear and yanked down. He shouted out in pain, and his attention diverted long enough for me to turn the tables and tackle him. He wouldn't get the best of me—not this time.

All the rage, frustration, and angst I'd felt boiled to the surface. I balled my fists and used his face as my own personal punching bag.

"This is for Lark!" I said. "And this is for Jack."

I grabbed my gun, pressed it into the center of his forehead, and said, "And this is for everyone who suffered because of you."

"Wait, please," he said. "Don't. I'm sorry."

"Georgiana!" Harvey said. "That's enough!"

I glanced over my shoulder. "No, it isn't! It will never be enough."

Harvey aimed his gun at Anthony, looked into my eyes, and said, "Back off. Come on, now. We got him. Lark is safe. Justice will be served. We'll make sure of it."

He'd get justice—a justice he didn't deserve. A lifetime of imprisonment without parole wasn't enough to undo the mental scars Lark would endure for years to come. I wanted to end his life as he'd ended Jack's. But it wouldn't bring Jack back, and it wouldn't change what he'd done to Lark. He was guilty of heinous acts, but he was the only parent Maya had left.

I eased the gun off his head and stood.

I wouldn't be responsible for taking him from Maya the way he'd taken Jack from Lark. No child deserved that, no matter how pathetic the parent.

Harvey bent over Anthony, slapped zip ties over his wrists, and lifted him off the ground.

Anthony looked up at him and said, "Thanks."

"Don't thank me," Harvey said. "I have half a mind to let her end your life, you son of a bitch."

46

"M ommy!" Lark screamed.

Face drenched in tears, Phoebe sprinted toward the Jeep, lifted Lark out of the passenger seat, and threw her arms around her, smothering her face in kisses.

"I missed you so much, honey," Phoebe said. "Are you all right?"

"Yeah, I think so. I want to go home. I want to see Willy. I miss him."

"Willy's here," Phoebe said. "Nanny picked him up today."

Lark's face lit up. "Can I see him, Mommy? Please?"

"You can do whatever you like, honey."

My mother, who had stood at the front door with my aunt and my brothers, exercising the most restraint I'd ever seen, reached a breaking point. She made a mad dash toward Lark, hollering words of gratitude toward the heavens the entire way. I couldn't help but smile. My family may not have been normal. Hell, I was far from it. But they were loyal, and they were mine.

Mom joined in on the group hug and said, "Nanny has your favorite ice cream in the freezer, Lark. How about we go make hot fudge sundaes?"

Lark nodded, Phoebe passed her off, and the two walked toward the front door.

Phoebe embraced me. Through staggered breaths, she said, "I can never thank you enough for bringing her back to me. I wish I could have done the same for you."

"I ... ahh ... you're welcome." For a time, we remained locked in an embrace, and then I said, "You have a daughter to spend time with, and I have a man to interrogate."

She released me and said, "I understand. Will you stop by after?"

I nodded. "There's no place I'd rather be."

Phoebe headed inside, and I stood there for a minute, watching her and Lark through the kitchen window, remembering a time I felt the same joy she was feeling now.

The front door opened, and my mother stepped out. I looked away and wiped a stray tear from my eye as she approached.

She squeezed my hand and said, "I'm proud of you. I know I don't say it enough, but I'm saying it now. You're an amazing woman, and I'm so grateful you're my daughter."

I couldn't recall the last time she'd spoken to me with such tenderness.

"Thanks, Mom."

"Won't you come inside? Lark would love to spend some time with you. We all would now that this is all over."

"I will," I said. "I just need to wrap up a few things at the station first."

"You're not, uh, leaving us again, are you?"

She looked worried, like she anticipated my answer, unsure of my reply.

"I'm staying," I said. "For now. I may even look into buying a place again. Not now, but sometime. We'll see how it goes."

I said goodbye and drove to the station. I walked to the interrogation room. Hunter was standing outside, watching the interview take place.

"How's it going in there?" I asked.

"Slow. Anthony Paine isn't in the mood to talk. Keeps asking for his lawyer."

"How long do we have?"

She checked the time on the clock on the wall. "His lawyer lives in King City. I'd guess thirty minutes."

Thirty minutes was enough.

"I wish I was more like you," she said. "You're assertive, and you have guts. I don't."

"You don't want to be like me," I said. "I make rash decisions sometimes, and I don't consider the consequences. I just act. You're more level-headed, which makes for a good detective."

"I'm not a good detective, though."

"You can be, if it's what you want."

"I'll miss working here, but I think I need to move on."

I respected her decision. "If you ever change your mind, and I'm still here, I'd be happy to teach you everything I know."

"Thanks, but I won't be coming back."

She tipped her head toward me and then walked down the hall. I opened the door to the interrogation room and stuck my head in.

"Mind if I talk to him for a few minutes?" I asked.

"No," Anthony said.

Harvey smiled. "Sure."

"No," Anthony said. "I'm not talking to her."

Harvey patted him on the shoulder, laughed, and said, "Good luck. You'll need it."

Then he exited the room.

I took a seat and paused a moment, thinking about the conversation I'd just had with Hunter and the labels I'd attached to myself.

"I've been to your house," I said. "I've seen the family photos. I know the kind of father you were to Maya, and the husband you were to Rebecca. You've never even had a speeding ticket before. Now that I'm sitting here looking at you, you don't look like a killer. You look like a decent guy. What happened?"

I knew what had happened.

I just wanted to hear him say it.

"Doesn't matter now, does it? I'm here. Rebecca's dead. And once my daughter hears about what I've done, she'll never see me the same way again."

"Maybe."

"What do you mean, *maybe*? She will."

"People can be understanding and forgiving when they want to be," I said. "It's all a matter of choice. You could choose to explain everything to me, and I could choose to help you with your daughter."

"I don't believe you."

"I've never gone back on my word. I don't plan to start now."

"What's the catch?"

"There isn't one. I just want to understand why you decided to do what you did."

I paused, giving him time to think.

He shook his head. "Nah, I'm not talking."

"Fine. Guess I'll spend the rest of my life making Maya part of my family until she's no longer interested in being part of yours."

"Do you always play dirty to get what you want?"

Not always.

"What I *want* is to rewind the clock to the night it all began. I want you to talk to Jack and decide not to kill him. I want my niece not to see what she saw, you not to take her, and her not have to spend the next several years of her life in therapy because of it ... because of *you*."

He huffed a heavy sigh. "I never meant ... She wasn't supposed to be part of it. I didn't even know he had a daughter."

"Think about how you'd feel if the same thing happened to Maya. I'm not asking you to feel remorse for what you did. Whether you do or don't, it doesn't make a difference. I'm asking for answers so I can help Lark's mother understand why you did what you did. She has an emotionally scarred daughter and a dead husband. She deserves to know the truth, your truth."

"She has a dead husband, and I have a dead wife."

"And a living daughter who loves you."

"She's my whole world, you know? At first, when Rebecca told me she planned to contact Maya's biological father, I thought I could handle it. And then I saw him with her at the party. I saw how fast they connected. I saw the way she looked at him. It was the same way she looked at me. I was already losing my wife. I couldn't lose my daughter too."

"When did you decide to kill him?"

"I didn't. I mean, I never thought it would go that far. I went to his house planning to talk, to explain to him that Maya was suffering over the loss of her mother. I thought if I told him, if I asked him to allow me to continue being the father I had always been, he would respect my position."

"What did he say?" I asked.

"He was sorry she was hurting, but he wanted to be part of her life. He suggested we help her through it together. I was outraged. He stepped in after eighteen years, having met her once, and tried to tell me we needed to share responsibility. *I* was her father. *I* was there when she had a broken bone and needed a shoulder to cry on. Not him."

"So, you decided to shoot him?"

"I didn't even think about it. I just did it. Once it happened, there was no going back. It was too late. And then I heard a little girl scream. I'm sure you won't believe me, but I never intended on taking her. I just … I couldn't leave her there knowing she'd seen what I'd done."

"What about Andy Sanders, the private investigator he hired?"

"I caught him following me a couple of days after Jack died. I figure he'd suspected what I'd done and was trying to get proof before he went to the police."

I'd heard all I needed to hear for now. The rest could wait until court. I scooted my chair back and stood.

"You will help me with my daughter like you said, won't you?"

I opened the door and stepped out. "Like I said, I always keep my word."

I returned to my office to grab my purse off my desk and encountered an unpleasant surprise. Mayor Wheeler had been sitting there, waiting.

"Mayor Wheeler," I said. "Is everything okay?"

He fiddled with his phone and said, "Did you get what you needed out of Mr. Paine?"

"I did."

"Good. I'd like to talk to you for a minute. I'm sure you're anxious to get back to your family. I won't take up too much of your time."

I leaned against the wall and crossed my arms. "Okay."

He peeled his eyes away from his phone and stared at my face.

"Nice shiner," he said. "You okay?"

"I'll survive."

"I heard about what happened today."

"Okay."

I flashed back to the moment my gun was pressed against Anthony's head, closed my eyes, and braced for the backlash to come.

"Great detective work," he said. "After the news broke that we had the perpetrator in custody, my phone didn't stop ringing. I'm being praised all around, but I'm not the one who deserves it. You do."

"I just did what anyone would in my position."

"Still, I wanted to stop by in person and let you know how thrilled I am to see this case solved."

It was no secret he hoped to be reelected the next year. Solving a murder-and-kidnapping case added a shinier feather to his cap.

"Thanks," I said. "Anything else?"

"You staying or going?"

"Staying, for now."

He stood. "Well, good. One thing, though. You, ehh … you might want to consider looking into anger management classes."

"Are you asking me or telling me?"

"Neither, at the moment. It's just a suggestion. Have a good night. Give that niece of yours a big squeeze. Because of you, she's back with her loved ones tonight."

He started for the door, and I said, "You're being more generous with me this evening than you have been. Does this mean we can start off with a clean slate?"

He looked back and shot me a wink. "Oh, I wouldn't go that far."

Three weeks later

I stood in front of the full-sized mirror, assessed my eighth wardrobe change, and decided it didn't matter what I wore tonight. I was nervous; I'd never be one hundred percent satisfied. I settled on a black, drop-waist, petal-style chiffon dress with sequin beading and matching round-toe, T-strap heels. I glanced at the time. My cab would be pulling up to the curb any minute.

I locked the door to the hotel room, took the elevator, and got into the cab. Several minutes later I was dropped in front of Osteria dei Mascalzoni. I walked inside and was greeted by a young man in a black suit.

"You must be Georgiana," he said.

"I am."

"I'm Sergio. Allow me to show you to your table."

We walked to the back of the dimly lit restaurant, and he sat me inside one of three private, booth-style, circular rooms with long, red, velvet drapes tied at each side.

Sergio unfastened the drapes, pulled them almost all the way closed, and said, "Giovanni will be here in a few minutes. May I offer you something to drink while you wait?"

"Can you make a Mary Pickford?"

"I can make anything."

He disappeared behind the curtain, and I sat back, fiddling with the beading on my dress and doing my best to calm my nerves. The curtain parted, and I looked up to see Giovanni smiling down on me. He set my cocktail on the table and spread his arms. I stood, and we embraced.

"It's like I just saw you yesterday," he said. "It feels like no time has passed."

I felt the same.

He took a step back and looked me over. "You look beautiful, and I see you haven't lost your love for vintage clothing." He sat beside me. "How's the little one doing?"

"Lark is all right. The first few days were the worst. She'd wake up crying, thinking she was back in the house she'd been kept in after she was taken, even though she was in bed next to my sister. We're all doing our best to help her get things back to the way they used to be. She's been playing a lot with Ethan, the boy who lives across the street. She's not back in school yet, but I think if we give her another week or two, she will be."

"Why isn't she in school?"

"She's had a lot of separation anxiety. She panics sometimes when Phoebe leaves the room."

He placed his hand on mine. "I don't know what I can do, but if there's anything at all, please tell me."

"Thank you. It's nice to be here, to put it all on pause for a moment. Before I came here, I went to see Maya, Jack's daughter. Like Lark, she's dealing with a lot too. She just lost her mother, and her father is headed to prison."

"How was she?"

"Fragile. At the moment, she refuses to see her father. I don't blame her. I shared my thoughts about why he did what he did. It doesn't make much of a difference to her now, but in time, I believe she'll come around and allow him in her life again. For now, I've told her about her half-sister Lark, and I invited her to come to Cambria to meet her and our family."

"Do you think she will?"

"I do."

Sergio walked in with two other men. He set a drink down beside Giovanni, and the men filled the table with more food than I could eat in a week. Then they turned and went without saying a word.

"Where are all the patrons?" I asked, realizing I hadn't seen another customer in the place.

"I closed the restaurant to host a private event."

"You didn't have to close it for me."

"I know I didn't. I wanted to do it. What will you do now that you've solved your case?"

"I'm not sure yet. It feels good to be in my home town again. What about you? Do you think you'll always stay in New York?"

"I will always consider New York my home, but there are many places I'd like to see. I don't want to live here. I want to live everywhere."

It sounded like the ideal life.

"Where are you off to next?" I asked.

"Machu Picchu in Peru. But first I have some business in Sicily."

"I've never been to Peru."

"You should come with me."

"Maybe I will."

Giovanni pointed to a dish in the center of the table.

"What is it?" I asked.

"Uova al cirighet. Fried eggs in a lemon sauce. It's my mother's recipe. Try it. Tell me what you think."

I scooped some onto a spoon and sampled what may have been one of the best egg dishes I'd ever had.

"It's amazing."

"I remember everything about the time we spent together in our younger years, including how often you cooked eggs."

We spent the next several minutes talking, savoring each dish, and sharing a bottle of wine. It was hard to believe a couple of hours earlier I'd fretted over seeing him again. Sitting there now, I was filled with a sense of ease. It was like we'd picked up right where we'd left off, and I didn't want the night to end.

"When are you going to Sicily?" I asked.

"In a few days from now. I won't be long, just a week or two. I'm taking care of a few things for Daniela."

"You know, in school I thought your family ... well, it's just ... there were times when I wondered if your family was tied to the mafia somehow."

He grabbed his glass, swilled a bit of wine, and set the glass back on the table. He seemed uncomfortable answering the question, but I was no longer good at tiptoeing around issues.

"Is your family in the mafia?" I asked.

"You're a smart woman, Gigi. You have good instincts about people. What are your instincts telling you now?"

His question was my answer.

"It's different than it used to be," he said. "It's much more civilized. My role is to help Daniela when she needs it. Nothing more. Do you think less of me for it?"

I didn't know.

I didn't think so.

"At the moment? No. I see you as I always have."

The one who got away.

"I have a question for you now," he said. "Why did you leave Cambria?"

I folded my arms and stared into my lap. "It's … something I don't like talking about."

"I hope you know you can tell me anything, but I won't press any further."

I knew I could tell him anything.

It was one of the things I liked most about him.

When we were together, I always felt safe.

"I had a daughter," I whispered. "Her name was Fallon."

Tears welled in my eyes, tears I didn't want to come but always did whenever I spoke her name. I wanted to keep my head down, to avoid eye contact, but I couldn't. I looked at him. Any resolve I'd had to contain myself melted away, and the floodgates opened.

He nodded and then said, "Come here."

I wrapped my arms around him, and he kissed my forehead. "It's okay, il mio cuore. It's okay."

I took the time to regain my composure, and then I leaned back.

"You don't have to discuss it if you don't want to, all right?" he said.

"I've never talked to anyone about what happened to her before. Sitting here now, I want it to be you."

He nodded and waited for me to begin.

"Fallon was three years old when she died. I was in the house, putting some clothes into the dryer. Frank Sinatra was playing on the record player. Fallon wanted to go swimming, and I promised we would after I finished a few chores around the house. She was impatient. I suppose she got that from me. I'd left her playing in the sandbox outside. It was a bit windier than I realized, and the door latch for the pool area came open. Fallon must have walked inside and jumped in. Because of how loud the music was, I didn't hear it. I don't know how to explain it, but standing in the laundry room, I felt something was wrong. A mother's intuition, I guess. I wasn't away from her for more than a few minutes, but by the time I walked back outside, it was too late."

He leaned forward, wrapped his hands around my arms, and said, "I'm sorry. You must know it wasn't your fault. It was an accident."

"*I* walked away. *I* left her alone. If I hadn't, she'd still be alive. She's dead because I was a bad parent. The day she died, I learned toddlers can drown in a pool in as little as twenty seconds. Because of my ignorance, she's dead."

I'd always thought talking about her death would make me feel worse. Reliving it now wasn't easy. But I also felt a sense of relief, like sharing it with him had relieved me of bearing the entire burden myself.

"Daniela isn't my only sister," he said. "I had another one. Her name was Viola. She was thirteen when she died."

"Can I ask what happened?"

He nodded. "I was fifteen. My parents were out of town. They'd left us with Flavia, our nanny. After Flavia went to bed, I found the keys to my father's Mercedes, and I took Daniela and Viola for a joyride. I never planned to go far, just a couple of blocks, but once I got behind the wheel, Daniela pushed me to see how fast it would go, and I was happy to oblige. I got it up to seventy-eight before I noticed the street ended with an abrupt cul-de-sac. I took my foot off the pedal and tried to make the turn, but it was too late. The car plowed into the side of a house. Daniela and I suffered a few scrapes and broken bones, but Viola was thrown from the car, and she died."

Shocked, I brought a hand to my chest. "I'm so sorry. I had no idea. Daniela never spoke of her."

"I haven't told that story for a long time, but hearing what you experienced and seeing the pain you carry, I knew you needed to hear it."

"I did. I'm glad you chose to share it with me."

"All of us bear scars in some form or another. What matters is learning to forgive yourself. We cannot change the past. What's done is done. But we can use the lessons we've learned to write the story of our future. You're a good person, Gigi. You need to forgive yourself."

Sergio returned to gather the plates, and Giovanni suggested we go for a walk before calling an end to the night. He draped his suit jacket over my shoulders, and we headed onto the street, taking in the sights, sounds, and smells that were the beauty of New York City.

The air seemed different tonight, and my breath felt different, like I was taking it in for the first time. I looked up at Giovanni, and he stared into my eyes like he read my thoughts. He leaned down, and we kissed.

When our lips parted, he said, "Thank you."

"For what?"

"For trusting me enough to share the most intimate part of your life, and for kissing me back. I've wanted to do that for twenty years."

THE END

Thank you for reading Little Girl Lost, book one in the Georgiana Germaine mystery series.

I hope you enjoyed getting to know the characters in Gigi's world as much as I have enjoyed writing them for you. This is a continuing series with more books coming after the one you just read. You can find the series order (as of the date of this printing) in the "Books by Cheryl Bradshaw" section below.

In Little Lost Secrets, Book 2 in the series, Georgiana is swept up in a cold case murder when a dead body is found within the walls during a home renovation. How did the body get there? And what ties does it have to Georgiana's father's death more than three decades earlier?

Here's an exclusive look at chapter one ...

It had been a long, arduous half hour for Tiffany Wheeler, and she feared it would get worse before it got better. Her boyfriend, Russell, stood a few feet away, his head cocked to the side, eyes wild. He brushed a lock of his black hair out of his eye, unbuttoned his suit jacket, and stared at her the way he always did right before his blood reached its boiling point and was about to bubble over.

"What do you mean you don't want to live in LA anymore?" he asked. "Why not?"

"I've already told you why," she said. "I'm tired of the fast-paced life. I want to move back home."

"You said you were coming here to do a few simple renovations to this house before you listed it. I get here and the place is a flipping disaster. You've torn down walls, gutted the kitchen. What gives?"

Tiffany remained quiet, considering the best way to proceed. It didn't matter what she said. Russell was used to getting his way, something he wouldn't get tonight.

He was in denial.

She was avoiding what had still been left unsaid.

Confrontation of any kind had always been difficult between them in the two years they'd been together. Russell was used to the high life, climbing the corporate ladder, and taking any steps necessary to rise to the top. In their relationship, it had always been his way or no way. And Tiffany now realized since they'd been together, she hadn't just lost her identity; she'd lost her voice.

I think we should break up were the words she needed to say.

Such simple words.

And yet, she struggled to bring herself to say them.

"I've decided to keep the house," she said. "And I think we should … it's just … I've done a lot of thinking since I've been here, and you're a good guy. But I don't think we're right for each other. I waited until tonight to tell you how I was feeling because I hoped the doubts I'd been having about our relationship would go away. They haven't, and I need to be honest … with you and with myself."

Russell clenched his jaw and stepped back. "What you're saying is, I'm a *good* guy, but not a *great* one. I'm good for you, just not good enough."

In a moment of childish defiance, he scooped the flowers he'd just given her off the counter and tossed them at her face.

"You want to tell me what's really going on here?" he barked. "You stepping out on me? Huh? You screwing somebody else?"

"Of course not!" she said. "Calm down. You're being irrational."

"You want irrational? I'll give you irrational. I planned on surprising you tonight." He reached a hand inside his pants pocket, pulled out ring, and shoved it in front of her face. "I was going to surprise you with this."

An engagement ring?

The subject of marriage had never even been discussed before.

"You were going to propose?" she asked.

He jerked his arm back and hurled the ring across the room, and she watched it disappear into a pile of drywall scraps.

"I *was* going to propose," he said. "Not anymore. I thought we felt the same way about each other. Turns out, I'm the idiot. I like you, and *you* like someone else."

"What are you talking …? I'm telling the truth. There is no one else."

"The least you could do is not lie to my face."

He pushed her to the side and stormed into the living room, crouching over the area where he'd tossed the ring. She bent down beside him, reaching a hand into the pile to assist. He grabbed her wrist and snapped it back.

"Don't," he said. "I don't want your help."

She ignored the comment and reached in again.

He flashed her an infuriated look and thrust a hand into her chest, hurtling her backward. Her head smacked against the wall behind her. Outraged by his physical assault, her first instinct was to shove him back, but when they locked eyes, the only thing she saw in his was pain—a man whose life had just crumbled to dust without any forewarning.

"I love you, Tiffany," he said. "I have no idea what I did to lose you, to deserve what you're putting me through right …"

He stared at the wall, allowing his words to trail off before balling his hands into fists. Not knowing what would come next, Tiffany said, "No, Russell. Whatever you're thinking of doing … don't."

She darted to the side. He drilled his fist into the wall inches from where her head had just been and then slumped to the ground beside her.

"I'm gutted," he whispered. "You've torn me in half tonight."

Tiffany exhaled a long breath of air and then placed a hand on his shoulder. She let it rest there for a moment, and then she crawled over to the pile of drywall. She ran her fingers through the scraps, searching for the ring. She found it and turned, holding the ring out in front of her.

"Here," she said. "Take it. Take it and go. Okay?"

She dropped the ring into his hand, and he nodded. He pushed himself off the floor and walked toward the front of the house, stopping to glance back at her one last time before he left.

"I feel like I have no idea who you are," he said. "The Tiffany I know shops at Gucci, stays in five-star hotels, and loves the energy and hustle of the city. This ... what you've got going here, it isn't you, and it will never work. Enjoy your crap life in your crap house."

He walked out, allowing the door to slam behind him. She went to the window, pushed the curtain to the side, and watched him tear into the night. The breakup had been much more bitter and raw than she'd expected. But she was certain she made the right choice, even though she was sickened by what had just transpired between them.

She slid the curtain closed, grabbed a bottle of red wine out of a cardboard box, and guzzled half of it down. The recent weeks of pent-up frustration came flooding back in a wave of tears. She set the bottle down and walked into the living room, staring at the hole Russell had left in the wall. She reached down and picked up the construction worker's sledgehammer, running its forged-steel head along her hand. She lugged the hammer behind her and swung at the wall, again and again and again, breaking the drywall, piece by infuriating piece. As her blows ripped the wall apart, her anger began to subside.

She dropped the hammer and fell to her knees, allowing weeks of repressed tears to flow. When her eyes opened again, she blinked into the hole she'd created, aghast to find she wasn't the only one taking up residence within the walls of the house. There, in the wall's hidden crevices, Tiffany made a gruesome discovery. Preserved in layers of dust-filled plastic were what appeared to be remains—*human* remains.

ABOUT CHERYL BRADSHAW

Cheryl Bradshaw is a *New York Times* and *USA Today* bestselling author writing in the genres of mystery, thriller, paranormal suspense, and romantic suspense, among others. Her novel *Stranger in Town* (Sloane Monroe series #4) was a 2013 Shamus Award finalist for Best PI Novel of the Year, and her novel *I Have a Secret* (Sloane Monroe series #3) was a 2013 eFestival of Words winner for Best Thriller. To date, almost a dozen of Cheryl's novels has made the *USA Today* bestselling books list.

BOOKS BY CHERYL BRADSHAW

Sloane Monroe Series

<u>Black Diamond Death</u> (Book 1)
Charlotte Halliwell has a secret. But before revealing it to her sister, she's found dead.

<u>Murder in Mind</u> (Book 2)
A woman is found murdered, the serial killer's trademark "S" carved into her wrist.

<u>I Have a Secret</u> (Book 3)
Doug Ward has been running from his past for twenty years. But after his fourth whisky of the night, he doesn't want to keep quiet, not anymore.

<u>Stranger in Town</u> (Book 4)
A frantic mother runs down the aisles, searching for her missing daughter. But little Olivia is already gone.

<u>Bed of Bones</u> (Book 5) (USA Today Bestselling Book)
Sometimes even the deepest, darkest secrets find their way to the surface.

<u>Flirting with Danger</u> (Book 5.5) A Sloane Monroe Short Story
A fancy hotel. A weekend getaway. For Sloane Monroe, rest has finally arrived, until the lights go out, a woman screams, and Sloane's nightmare begins.

<u>Hush Now Baby</u> (Book 6) (USA Today Bestselling Book)
Serena Westwood tiptoes to her baby's crib and looks inside, startled to find her newborn son is gone.

<u>Dead of Night</u> (Book 6.5) A Sloane Monroe Short Story
After her mother-in-law is fatally stabbed, Wren is seen fleeing with the bloody knife. Is Wren the killer, or is a dark, scandalous family secret to blame?

<u>Gone Daddy Gone</u> (Book 7) (USA Today Bestselling Book)
A man lurks behind Shelby in the park. Who is he? And why does he have a gun?

<u>Smoke & Mirrors</u> (Book 8) (USA Today Bestselling Book)
Grace Ashby wakes to the sound of a horrifying scream. She races down the hallway, finding her mother's lifeless body on the floor in a pool of blood. Her mother's boyfriend Hugh is hunched over her, but is Hugh really her mother's killer?

Sloane Monroe Stories: Deadly Sins

<u>Deadly Sins: Sloth</u> (Book 1)
Darryl has been shot, and a mysterious woman is sprawled out on the floor in his hallway. She's dead too. Who is she? And why have they both been murdered?

Addison Lockhart Series

Grayson Manor Haunting (Book 1)
When Addison Lockhart inherits Grayson Manor after her mother's untimely death, she unlocks a secret that's been kept hidden for over fifty years.

Rosecliff Manor Haunting (Book 2)
Addison Lockhart jolts awake. The dream had seemed so real. Eleven-year-old twins Vivian and Grace were so full of life, but they couldn't be. They've been dead for over forty years.

Blackthorn Manor Haunting (Book 3)
Addison Lockhart leans over the manor's window, gasping when she feels a hand on her back. She grabs the windowsill to brace herself, but it's too late--she's already falling.

Belle Manor Haunting (Book 4)
A vehicle barrels through the stop sign, slamming into the car Addison Lockhart is inside before fleeing the scene. Who is the driver of the other car? And what secrets within the walls of Belle Manor will provide the answer?

Till Death do us Part Novella Series

Whispers of Murder (Book 1)
It was Isabelle Donnelly's wedding day, a moment in time that should have been the happiest in her life...until it ended in murder.

<u>Echoes of Murder</u> (Book 2)
When two women are found dead at the same wedding, medical examiner Reagan Davenport will stop at nothing to discover the identity of the killer.

Stand-Alone Novels

<u>Eye for Revenge</u> (USA Today Bestselling Book)
Quinn Montgomery wakes to find herself in the hospital. Her childhood best friend Evie is dead, and Evie's four-year-old son witnessed it all. Traumatized over what he saw, he hasn't spoken.

<u>The Perfect Lie</u>
When true-crime writer Alexandria Weston is found murdered on the last stop of her book tour, fellow writer Joss Jax steps in to investigate.

<u>Hickory Dickory Dead</u> (USA Today Bestselling Book)
Maisie Fezziwig wakes to a harrowing scream outside. Curious, she walks outside to investigate, and Maisie stumbles on a grisly murder that will change her life forever.

<u>Roadkill</u> (USA Today Bestselling Book)

Suburban housewife Juliette Granger has been living a secret life ... a life that's about to turn deadly for everyone she loves.

Made in the USA
Middletown, DE
07 February 2022

60694003R00149